Stories, sayings, and Scriptures to Encourage and Inspire

“拥抱·爱”系列双语典藏读物

hugs™ for Scrapbookers

附赠 CD

心情涂鸦

Stephanie Howard
LeAnn Weiss 著

方华文 主 译
鲍 曼 贺爱军
陈 民 刘 滨 译
袁 满

安徽科学技术出版社
HOWARD BOOKS

[皖]版贸登记号:1208543

图书在版编目(CIP)数据

拥抱·爱.心情涂鸦:英汉对照/(美)霍华德(Howard,S.),(美)韦斯(Weiss,L.)著;方华文主译.—合肥:安徽科学技术出版社,2009.1
ISBN 978-7-5337-4269-0

Ⅰ.拥… Ⅱ.①霍…②韦…③方… Ⅲ.①英语-汉语-对照读物②故事-作品集-美国-现代 Ⅳ.H319.4:Ⅰ

中国版本图书馆 CIP 数据核字(2008)第198272号

拥抱·爱.心情涂鸦:英汉对照
(美)霍华德(Howard,S.)(美)韦斯(Weiss,L.)著 方华文 主译

出 版 人:黄和平
责任编辑:姚敏淑 余登兵
封面设计:朱 婧
出版发行:安徽科学技术出版社(合肥市政务文化新区圣泉路1118号出版传媒广场,邮编:230071)
电 话:(0551)3533330
网 址:www.ahstp.net
E - mail:yougoubu@sina.com
经 销:新华书店
排 版:安徽事达科技贸易有限公司
印 刷:合肥晓星印刷有限责任公司
开 本:787×1240 1/32
印 张:6.5
字 数:83千
版 次:2009年1月第1版 2009年1月第1次印刷
印 数:6 000
定 价:16.00元

(本书如有印装质量问题,影响阅读,请向本社市场营销部调换)

给爱一个归宿
——出版者的话

身体语言是人与人之间最重要的沟通方式，而身体失语已让我们失去了很多明媚的“春天”，为什么不可以给爱一个形式？现在就转身，给你爱的人一个发自内心的拥抱，你会发现，生活如此美好！

肢体的拥抱是爱的诠释，心灵的拥抱则是情感的沟通，彰显人类的乐观坚强、果敢执著与大爱无疆。也许，您对家人、朋友满怀缱绻深情却羞于表达，那就送他一本《拥抱·爱》吧。一本书，七个关于真爱的故事；一本书，一份荡涤尘埃的“心灵七日斋”。一个个叩人心扉的真实故事，一句句震撼心灵的随笔感悟，从普通人尘封许久的灵魂深处走出来，在洒满大爱阳光的温情宇宙中尽情抒写人性的光辉！

“拥抱·爱”(Hugs)系列双语典藏读物是“心灵鸡汤”的姊妹篇，安徽科学技术出版社与美国出版巨头西蒙舒斯特携手倾力打造，旨在把这套深得美国读者青睐的畅销书作为一道饕餮大餐，奉献给中国的读者朋友们。

每本书附赠CD光盘一张，纯正美语配乐朗诵，让您在天籁之音中欣赏精妙美文，学习地道发音。

世界上最遥远的距离，不是树枝无法相依，而是相互凝望的星星却没有交会的轨迹。

“拥抱·爱”系列双语典藏读物，助您倾吐真情、启迪心智、激扬人生！

一本好书一生财富，今天你拥抱了吗？

Contents

For Ryan, Asa,
Aslyn, and Aevin.
You are the greatest
scrapbook material!
I love you!

Chapter 1

Staying Connected

1 保持联系

You're unforgettable to Me. I've engraved you on the very palms of my hands. I'll never leave you or abandon you. You can always count on My unconditional love and goodness.

Eternal hugs,
Your Heavenly Father

—from Isaiah 49:16; Deuteronomy 31:6; Psalm 23:6

我不会忘记你。我已将你铭刻在我掌心。我永远不离不弃你。我一生一世绝对会关爱与保佑你。

永远拥抱你，
你在天上的父

——《以赛亚书》49:16；
《申命记》31:6；
《诗篇》23:6

Have you ever noticed the immediate connection you have with someone once you learn that she scrapbooks too? With that discovery two strangers instantly connect. Suddenly they have plenty to talk about. "How many books do you have?" "How often do you work on them? "What kind of journaling do you do?"

There are so many things to ask and learn from a fellow scrapbooker, and it's quite likely that the conversation will end with an invitation to work on albums together in the future. Many new friendships have formed in the process of sharing ideas and trying new techniques. It's not unusual to find that as you craft your pages and memories together, you're crafting relationships and sharing joys.

Scrapbooking with

others is a great way to stay connected too. Often we get so busy taking care of our families and their busy schedules that it's hard to find time for friends. Sometimes the only opportunity we have to catch up with them is when we get together to work on our albums. Friends can work side by side, arranging their favorite photos while catching up on the happenings in each other's lives.

Scrapbook albums help us stay connected here and now, and they help us stay connected to our past as family and friends relive their adventures and strengthen their ties with us any time we flip through the pages. And scrapbooking also helps us connect with others to enrich our future.

Aren't you glad you're connected?

你可曾注意到？一旦你得知某人也制作剪贴簿，即刻你们的距离就被拉近了。由于那个发现，两个陌生人顷刻间心灵无间。突然间，他们就有如此多的共同话题。"你有多少本剪贴簿了？""你多久制作一次？""你制作什么种类的剪贴簿？"

从制作剪贴簿的同盟者那里，你可以询问和得知如此多的事情，并且极有可能随着谈话的结束，伴随而来的是一份关于在一起做相册的邀请。许多新的友谊在分享好主意和竭力尝试新的制作技巧的过程中建立了起来。这并不平常，当你发现你巧妙地将每一个页面和每一点回忆制作在一起时，你也精雕细琢了你们之间的友谊，分享了其中的乐趣。

和他人一起做剪贴簿也是一个很棒的保持联系的方

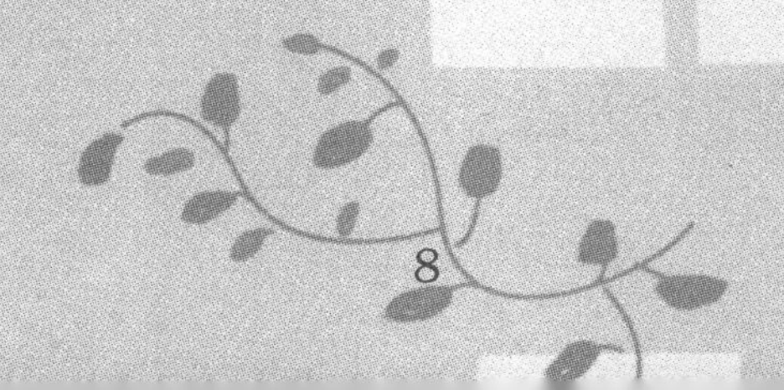

法。平日里我们总是忙碌于照料家人，接受他们的日程安排，因此难以为朋友们空出时间。有时候我们可以抓住和他们在一起仅有的机会就是当我们聚在一起为了剪贴簿而工作的时候。朋友之间可以肩并肩，整理他们最中意的照片，同时会因彼此生活中的亮点而着迷。

不论在何时，当我们草草翻阅每一个页面，相册剪贴簿都会帮助我们保持联系，不仅仅是在当前，也会让我们同过去时光保持联系，当家庭成员和朋友们重温他们的冒险生活，这些都加强了与我们的联系。剪贴簿也帮助我们同他人建立联系，从而使我们的未来更加丰富。

难道你不为自己有他人惦记而开心么?

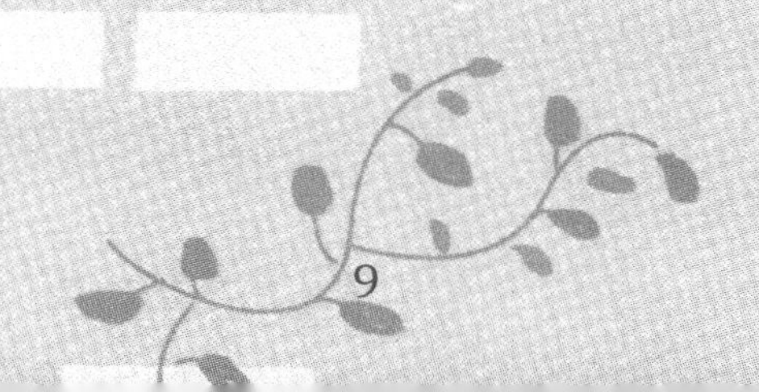

There can be no happiness equal
to the joy of finding a heart
that understands.
Victor Robinson

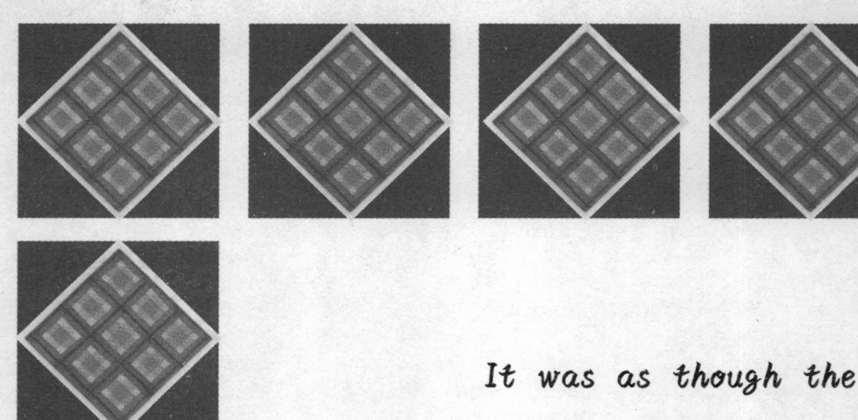

It was as though the
final thread had
been severed. Tessa
was'nt sure she
could keep this up.

Thursdays with Ina

"Hey, Tessa! I've been looking for you." Tessa had just locked her dorm room when she saw her friend Pam coming down the hall.

"Hi, Pam. What's up?"

"A bunch of girls are going to a movie tonight. You want to come?"

Tessa crinkled her nose apologetically. "Sorry, not tonight. I was just leaving to scrapbook with Ina." Tessa had a standing appointment with her grandmother most Thursday evenings.

"Oh, that's right. I forgot it's Thursday. How's she doing these days?"

Tessa smiled even as she felt a twinge of discouragement. "As well as can be expected. Some days are better than others."

Ina had Alzheimer's disease. For a while Tessa's family had taken Ina into their home. But when Ina started wandering in the middle of the night and taking extra doses of medicine, the family had made the difficult decision to place her in a nursing home.

Now, every available Thursday evening, Tessa packed up her scrapbook supplies and went to visit Ina. Unfortunately, Ina's illness had slowly stolen her ability to enjoy most of her favorite leisure activities, but she still showed interest in scrapbooking—even if she sometimes mixed things up or forgot what she was working on. Reviving their shared hobby was Tessa's effort to help Ina remember things through family photos.

Ina had stopped recognizing her granddaughter a few months ago. Although Tessa had known to expect this, it still felt disconcerting. That was one of the reasons she called her grandmother by her first name. Sometimes Ina's confusion caused her to become agitated when she didn't recognize family members. It just seemed easier to avoid that if possible.

Tessa felt strongly about continuing their hobby together, about trying to preserve some sense of connection, but as Ina's memory deteriorated, their meetings seemed to have little purpose. It was as though the final thread had been severed, and terrible as she knew the thought was, Tessa wasn't sure she could keep this up.

She arrived at Ina's room just after the dinner hour. It was a small space, yet cozy. Besides the green recliner, a bed and dresser were the only other pieces of furniture. The window valance and bed-spread were of the green toile fabric Ina had chosen and sewn herself years ago to complement her favorite chair. Tessa and her family had tried to bring as much familiarity to Ina's new surroundings as possible.

Knocking on the open door, she greeted Ina

with carefully constructed cheerfulness. "Hi, Ina! " The tiny but spry woman was seated in her green recliner, watching a bird perched outside the window.

Ina turned to see her visitor. "Well, hello, dear. Have you brought my supper?"

"No, Ina, supper is over," Tessa explained patiently. She motioned to her scrapbook tote. "I've come to show you my scrapbook. I thought maybe you could help me with my pictures today."

With a look of pure delight, Ina stood up and welcomed Tessa into her room. "I would love to! "

Tessa smiled. One thing Ina hadn't lost was her enthusiasm.

Then Ina placed her hand on Tessa's shoulder. "I seem to have forgotten your name, dear."

Tessa swallowed, frustrated that she'd been caught off-guard again. Their re-introduction had become part of the routine. She should have been expecting this. "I'm Tessa, your granddaughter."

Ina seemed confused but not bothered by her

failed memory. "OK, Tessa."

Tessa laid the scrapbook on the bed. While Ina flipped through the pages, Tessa set up the rest of her scrapbook materials.

"This is lovely! " Ina exclaimed, admiring pages she herself had helped create. "Now, who is this?" She pointed to a photo of a man and woman holding hands.

"That's your daughter Gloria and her husband, Jim—my parents."

For a moment Ina gazed at the couple as if trying to find some missing link that would explain these strangers. Apparently unsuccessful, she simply tapped the photo and spoke matter-of-factly. "Well, they make a handsome couple. The young woman is quite pretty, don't you think? I like the mischief in her smile." She chuckled, revealing that same impish grin.

Tessa smiled and laughed. "Yes, she is." Taking her grandmother's thin, wrinkled hand, she caressed it tenderly. So much of Ina's life seemed lost, yet she somehow maintained a spark of vitality.

Ina looked at her. "What are you working on today, Ruth?" Ruth was Ina's sister, who had died when she was fifteen. Tessa tried to ignore the mistake. She opened an envelope and brought out a stack of photos from her camping trip with friends.

"We had a great time on this trip," Tessa explained as she pointed to a photo of her friend Pam sleeping alone in a large tent. "We played a joke on Pam because she wouldn't stop snoring. Before she woke up that morning, we all snuck out of the tent and arranged our sleeping bags twenty feet away from the camp, then pretended to be asleep. When she woke up and found us, we told her we'd slept outside all night because of her loud snoring! It was pretty funny."

Ina laughed heartily. "Oh, Tessa, you've always been such a comic! You get that from my side of the family, you know. We were always playing tricks and jokes on each other."

Tessa was too stunned to respond right away.

She glanced up at her grandmother's face just in time to see the brief moment of clarity before it faded.

Tessa turned her face slightly and averted her gaze to hide the tears that had sprung to her eyes. *She remembered.* Somewhere in that fog was her grandmother, the one who remembered and loved her.

Side by side the women worked and laughed. Tessa gave Ina some stickers of bonfires and camp paraphernalia to place throughout the two-page spread.

As Tessa finished journaling the high points of her trip, one of the nurse's aides came in to check on Ina and noticed their project. "Wow! That looks great!"

"Oh!" Ina said, looking at the scrapbook pages she'd just been working on as if for the first time. "Isn't it lovely!"

Tessa observed the look of happiness in her grandmother's eyes and had to force down the lump in her throat that made her smile quiver. Reaching for her bag, she turned to the nurse's aide. "Will you please take our picture?"

"Absolutely," the aide replied, gladly accepting the camera.

Cheek to cheek, the two women posed and smiled broadly, once for a close-up and once with their masterpiece. Ina likely wouldn't remember this day, but Tessa would never forget.

"Thanks," Tessa said to the aide. "I can't wait to show her these next Thursday."

艾娜的星期四

“嗨,蒂莎!我正找你呢。”蒂莎刚刚将自己寝室的门锁上,就看见自己的朋友帕姆出现在走廊上。

“嗨,帕姆。有事吗?”

“今晚许多女生一起去看电影,你也去么?”

蒂莎抱歉地皱了皱鼻子。“很抱歉,今晚不行。我刚刚把剪贴簿留给艾娜。”蒂莎几乎每个星期四的晚上都和祖母有个例行的约会。

“嗯,知道了。我忘记今天是星期四了。她最近如何?”

一阵阵遗憾刺痛着蒂莎,但微笑自始至终浮现在她脸上。“还是值得期待的。她的情况总是时好时坏。”

艾娜患了阿尔察默病。蒂莎一家把艾娜接到了家里。但是当艾娜开始在夜半时分徘徊,且开始服用超剂量的药物时,全家人做出

了异常艰难的决定，把艾娜安置在私人疗养院。

现在每个星期四晚上，只要有空，蒂莎就会整理好剪贴簿去看艾娜。非常不幸，艾娜的病情悄悄偷走了大部分她热衷的休闲活动的能力。但是她仍然对剪贴簿表现出浓厚的兴趣——即使她不时弄混一些事情或是忘记她正在做什么。蒂莎竭尽全力想通过家庭成员们的照片帮助艾娜记起一些事情，从而唤醒她们共同的爱好。

几个月前，艾娜就已经认不出自己的孙女了。尽管蒂莎早就知道这一刻会到来，但这还是让她不知所措。这也是她用祖母的名字称呼祖母的原因之一。艾娜有时思维混乱，无法认清家庭成员，这些都让她变得容易激动。如果条件允许，这一切仿佛很容易避免。

蒂莎坚信一起继续她俩的爱好，可以竭力保存“联系”的感觉，但随着艾娜记忆力的破坏，她们的约会似乎变得毫无目的。就像最后一根线已被剪断，但她知道这种想法很可怕，蒂莎对能否继续下去也没把握。

晚餐时间刚过，蒂莎就到了艾娜的房间。房间不大，却很舒适。除去绿色的躺椅，床和梳妆台就是仅有的家具了。窗帘和床单都是绿色棉制印花的，是多年前艾娜自己选择的布料和花型并亲手缝制的，为的是让自己最喜欢的椅子躺起来更舒服。蒂莎和其他家庭成员尽其所能将艾娜熟悉的器物尽可能多地带到她所处的新环境中。

敲敲开着的门，蒂莎向艾娜问好，并没表现出很高兴。“你好，艾娜！”艾娜身体瘦小，精神却很好，她正躺在绿色的躺椅中，注视着窗外一只栖息在树上的小鸟。

艾娜扭头看了看来访者。“噢，你好，亲爱的，你把我的晚餐送来了？”

“不，艾娜，你吃过晚餐了。”蒂莎耐心地解释着。她注意到自己背着的剪贴簿。“我到这儿来给你看看我的剪贴簿。我想今天或许你可以帮我整理整理照片。”

艾娜带着一脸纯粹的快乐，从躺椅中起身，将蒂莎迎进自己的房间。“我很乐意！”

蒂莎笑意盈盈。至少有一样艾娜还没有失去，那就是热情。

接着，艾娜将手轻抚着蒂莎的肩膀。“我好像记不起你的名字了，亲爱的。”

蒂莎克制着自己，她再次毫无防备地被挫败了。每次两人见面，互相介绍已经成为例行程序的一部分。她早应该知道这一刻的到来。“我是蒂莎，您的孙女儿。”

艾娜衰退的记忆让她有点儿困惑，但并没有表现出厌烦。“是的，蒂莎。”

蒂莎将剪贴簿放在床上。艾娜快速翻开几页，蒂莎把剪贴薄的剩下的页面全打开了。

“这太可爱了！”艾娜大呼，为她参与创作完成的页面感到自豪。“哦，这是谁？”她指着一张照片，照片里的一男一女十指相扣。

“是您的女儿歌莉娅和她的丈夫吉米，他们是我的父母。”

有那么一会儿，艾娜凝视着这对夫妻，仿佛在竭力搜寻某种被她遗忘的纽带，而这纽带可以表明这对陌生人和她之间的关系。但这种努力显然不成功，她只是轻轻敲了敲照片，就事论事地说了一些话。“喔，他们真是一对佳偶。年轻的女人非常漂亮，难道你不这么认为吗？我喜欢她恶作剧似的微笑。”她哧哧地笑出声，展露出与照片中相似的、顽皮的漏齿一笑。

蒂莎先是微笑，终于忍不住大笑起来。“是的，她当然很漂亮。”握起祖母干瘦、密布皱纹的手，她体贴地抚摸着。艾娜生命中的许多片段都已经被遗忘，但不知何故她却可以顽强地保存只剩下一点点的生命力。

艾娜看着蒂莎。“今天你在做什么，露丝？”露丝是艾娜的姐姐，早在艾娜15岁的时候就已经去世了。蒂莎刻意忽视了这个误会。她打开一个信封，取出一沓照片，照片中的她正和朋友们在野营。

“这次旅行，我们度过了非常棒的时光，”蒂莎详述着当时的情况，她指着一张朋友帕姆的照片，照片中的帕姆一个人睡在一个巨大的帐篷中。“我们和帕姆开了个玩笑，因为她不住地打鼾。那天早晨在她醒来之前，我们全都轻手轻脚地溜出了帐篷，且将我们的睡袋都安放在离露营地20英尺的地方，然后全部假装在睡觉。当她醒来找到我们的时候，我们告诉她整晚我们都睡在帐篷外面，全都是因为她巨大的鼾声。真是有趣极了。”

艾娜开怀大笑。“噢，蒂莎，你总表现得像个喜剧演员。你是从我家族那一脉继承了喜剧天分，你该明白的。过去我们总是互相搞恶作剧和开玩笑。”

蒂莎惊呆了，一时间竟不知道怎么应答艾娜的话。她立刻抬头注视祖母的面容，瞧见了祖母那片刻的清醒，但却稍纵即逝了。

蒂莎眼里噙满了泪水，她把脸转向一边，试图不让艾娜看到她在哭。她记起来了，在心灵迷雾中的某个地方，她的祖母仍旧记得她，且深爱着她。

蒂莎和祖母肩并肩地坐着，一起制作，一起开怀大笑。蒂莎递给艾娜一些有关篝火和露营行装的即时贴，以便能充实两个页面。

蒂莎停住了有关旅行的精彩瞬间的回顾，这时一位看护人员走进来，检查了一下艾娜的身体，并且注意到了她俩完成的工作。“哇！看起来太棒了。”

“哦！”艾娜说，她看着自己刚刚辛勤忙碌着的剪贴簿的页面，仿佛是第一次做这件事。“它有趣极了，不是吗？”

蒂莎留意了祖母眼中的快乐之情，不得不强压住自己的哽咽，这使她咯咯笑。蒂莎拿起自己的包，转向护理师。“给我们拍张照片可以么？”

“当然可以，”护理师回答，很开心地接过照相机。

脸贴着脸，两个女人摆着各种姿势，开怀地大笑，一会儿给个特写，一会儿来个经典造型。艾娜可能不会记得今天，但是蒂莎永远也不会忘记这个日子。

“谢谢，”蒂莎对护理师说。“我迫不及待想在下个星期四向她展示这些。”

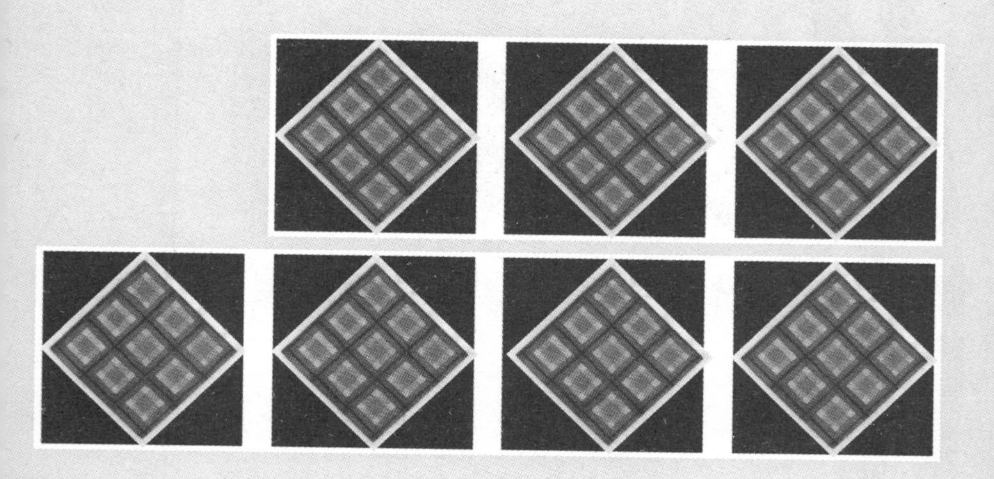

Chapter 2

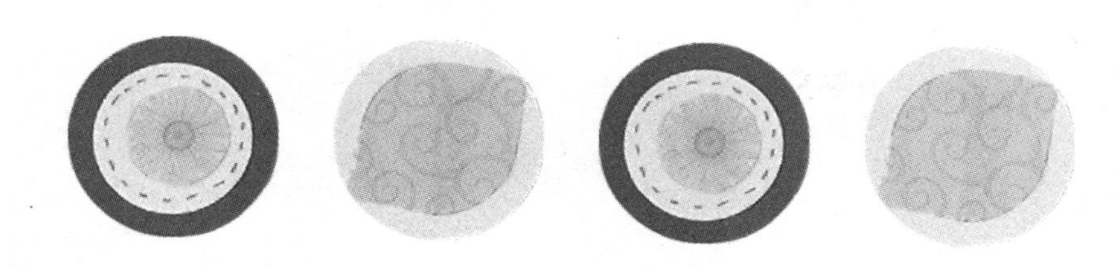

Bringing Healing

2 让心灵痊愈

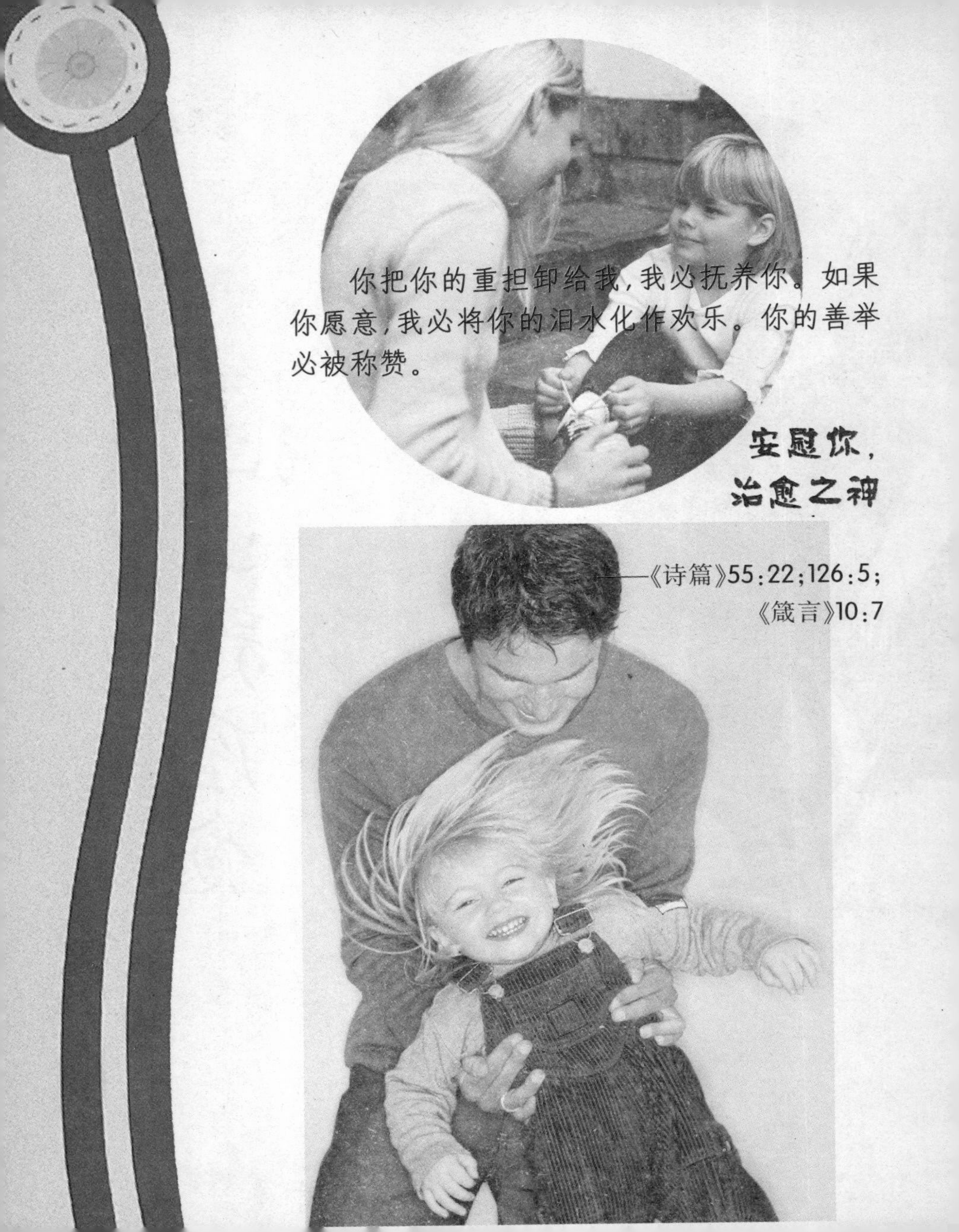

你把你的重担卸给我，我必抚养你。如果你愿意，我必将你的泪水化作欢乐。你的善举必被称赞。

安慰你，治愈之神

——《诗篇》55:22；126:5；《箴言》10:7

Give me the things that burden you, and I'll sustain you. Over time I'll transform your tears to joy, if you'll let me. You'll discover that the memory of the righteous truly is a blessing.

Comforting you,
The God Who Heals

—from Psalms 55:22; 126:5; Proverbs 10:7

Creating a scrapbook is valuable in so many ways. For one person it can be a relaxing activity. For another it might energize and inspire the imagination. Making a scrapbook can help build your own self-esteem or be used to encourage someone else. Any time energy is focused into a productive project, you're doing something good for yourself—and probably for others too.

Reminiscing is good for the soul. Just taking time out to remember what you did last summer or who came to last year's Christmas party can be a positive, enriching experience. It's fun to look back to see what has changed and what hasn't.

One of the most remarkable things about scrapbooks is that they can help people

Memories

inspirational message

heal. Whether you're creating a scrapbook or just reminiscing, the pages often hold a therapeutic, healing power.

A scrapbook can help someone who is grieving. While the pain of losing a loved one never goes away, remembering special moments with that person can help lessen feelings of loss. Although nothing can replace the unique presence of those we love, photos enable us to remember, celebrate, and communicate to others the impression they made on our lives. We can "bring back" lost loved ones just by remembering and reliving the good times we shared with them.

Reflecting on the past can be bittersweet, but it's the kind of pain that brings healing, peace, and restoration.

从许多方面来看，制作一本剪贴簿都是一件非常有意义的事情。对一些人来说这是一项让人放松的活动。对另外一些人来说，它可以让人思维活跃且可以激发想象力。制作一本剪贴簿可以帮助你建立自信心或是可以用来激励其他人。任何时候活力都可以聚焦成一项富有成效的工程,你正在做一件对自己很有意义的事情——可能对他人来说也是一样。

回忆对心灵不无裨益。仅仅是拿出时间去记住去年夏天你做了什么或是去年的圣诞节宴会谁到场了，这些都是积极的状态，丰富你的人生经历。回首看看哪些事情有了改变，哪些事情毫发未损，这些都有趣得很。

有关剪贴簿的最无法忽略的意义莫过于它们可以帮助人们疗伤。无论你是否正在做

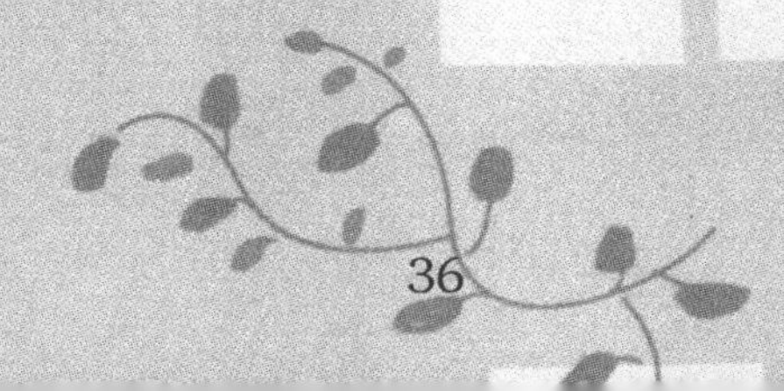

一本剪贴簿，抑或仅仅是回忆而已，剪贴簿中的一页页都承载了疗伤和治愈的力量。

剪贴簿可以帮助正在悲痛的人。当失去爱人的心碎之痛久久无法消散，牢记下和爱人在一起的特殊时刻，可以帮助减轻失去爱人的痛苦。尽管没有任何事情可以代替世界上那些我们深爱的独一无二的人的存在，照片却让我们铭记、赞美和与那些在我们生命中留下了浓墨重彩的人交流。我们能够“带回”失去的挚爱，仅仅通过回忆和再次体验我们和他们共享的美好时光就可以了。

细细回想过去的一切，有点儿苦涩的甜蜜，但这是一种苦药，可以让你的心灵痊愈，为你带来心灵的平和，让你的心灵复位。

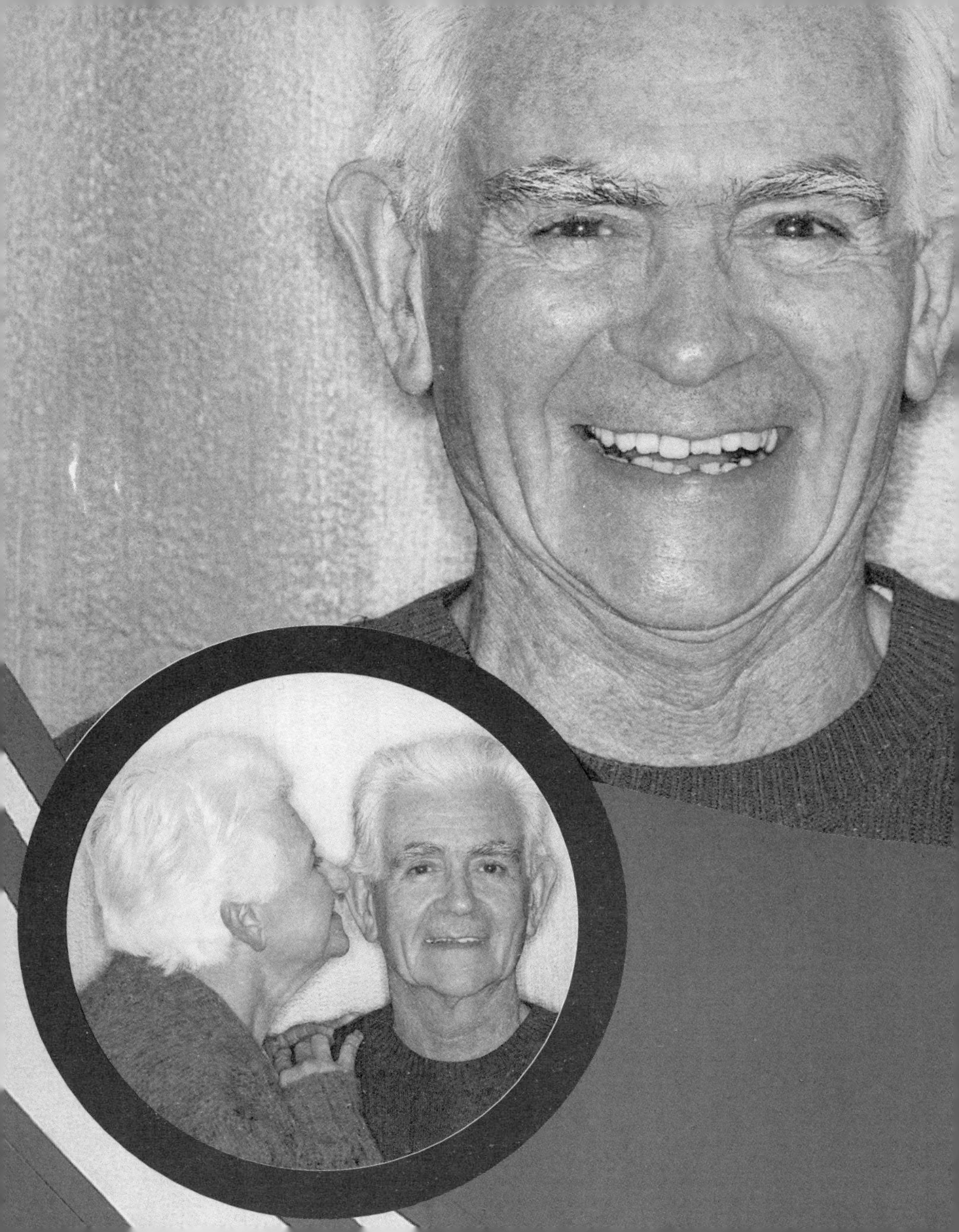

The only feelings
that do not heal
are the ones you hide.
Henri Nouwen

Sherry gasped as

she turned the

pages and saw

pictures she'd

never seen before.

Moving On

Sherry stood in front of the row of identical doors and heaved a sigh. Orange paint peeled off the storage building in random patterns. "What a run-down and dreary place," she muttered to no one.

Not that it made much difference. She planned to be surrounded by enough piles to block out her surroundings. Key in hand, Sherry opened the padlock and yanked on the door handle, waiting as the gray, metal panels rolled up out of the way.

Early morning sunlight spread quickly into the small room, casting shadows on the back wall. Sherry surveyed the large number of boxes piled almost to the ceiling and for a moment had second thoughts about conquering the task at hand. *Good thing Mom only had a two-bedroom duplex.* Her mother had always told her she tried to tackle too much at one time, but today she was determined to get through this unpleasant task.

Almost a year had passed since her mother died suddenly from a brain aneurysm, leaving Sherry stunned and emotionally immobilized. Her mother had always been her best friend, and her absence left a huge hole in Sherry's life. At the time she was barely able to handle the funeral arrangements, much less sorting and dispersing her mother's belongings. Her only sibling, Ben, lived overseas and had only been able to come home briefly for the funeral. Her husband, Joe, had suggested storing her mom's belongings until she was ready to go through everything.

Sherry told herself that she was as ready as she'd ever be. She'd willed herself to keep moving through the shock and denial immediately after her mother's death, though she still couldn't shake the anger. Some days she was so angry she didn't even want to shake it. She felt cheated—her mom had been only sixty-four years old. Her rational mind knew there was nothing she could have done to predict or prevent what had happened, but she was still mad at herself for not being more attentive to her mother's health. She was angry with her mother for leaving, even though she knew that made no sense. She was angry at her brother for not being more available right after their mother's death, when she needed him most. Today she was furious to be stuck—again—dealing with the aftermath alone. And she was angry with herself for being angry with those she loved. Sometimes it felt like the guilt was the only thing that checked her growing bitterness.

But as she stood facing the daunting task of sorting through her mother's belongings, a new wave of resentment washed away even the guilt and brought back fresh anger. *Fine!* she thought. *I'll just get this over with.*

Pushing up her sleeves, Sherry started shuffling

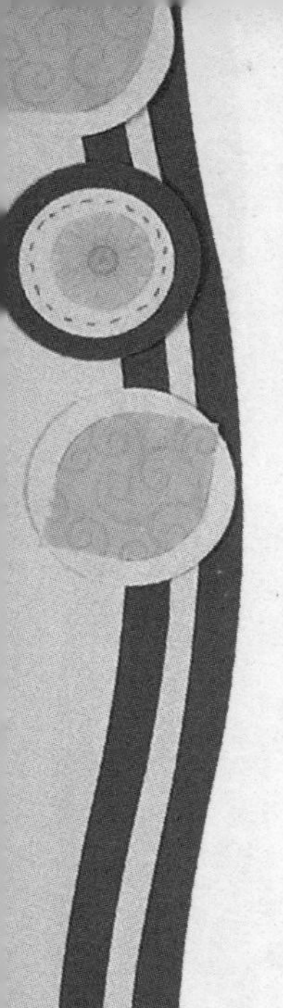

and slamming boxes marked "books" and "tax records" and "clothes" without even opening them. Adrenaline spurred her on for about a half-hour. She slowed down a little and was more careful with the boxes marked "china" and "decorations," looking inside long enough to pull out anything she wanted to keep as a memento but not long enough to let her emotions get the best of her again.

The next box was "gardening." Her mother had loved to garden and always had a plethora of seeds and how-to guides and tools. Maybe she would keep those. But she couldn't look at them. She added the box to the modest "keep" pile.

An unlabeled box caught Sherry's attention. *Great. Probably a bunch of miscellaneous junk.* She made a few hasty slices through the packing tape. Old crochet supplies. Her mother had tried the craft but never really took to it. Sherry started to put it in the pile to donate, but when she lifted it, it seemed heavier than it should for a bunch of yarn and some guide pamphlets. *That's odd.* She set the box down again and reached inside to rummage around.

Something solid was at the bottom, and she pulled out a large black book she didn't recognize. Her pace slowed as she noted the worn leather cover. Carefully, she opened the book and discovered what must have been her mother's childhood scrapbook. Sherry gasped as she turned the pages and saw pictures she'd never seen before. She unfolded an old newspaper clipping announcing her mother the winner of a county-fair beauty pageant. Another page displayed an eighth-grade report card with "Outstanding" written in the area reserved for comments. She couldn't read the others—tears were blurring her vision.

"Ugh…I thought I was through with this," Sherry muttered as she briskly wiped her eyes with her sleeve. But it was no use. Fresh tears were coming before she could even turn the page. For the first time in months, she felt a chink in her armor of selfprotective anger. She cleared a space on the floor and sat down with the scrapbook.

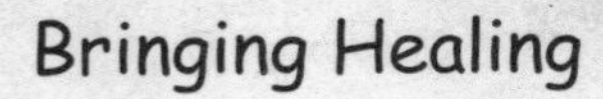

For the next hour, Sherry went through the pages, lingering over every image of her mother. She traced a finger along the edges of a photograph taken long ago and laughed aloud. It was a picture of her mother in her early teens, wearing a large, silly hat and puckering her lips dramatically for the camera. It perfectly captured the fun-loving spirit her mother had always had.

Sherry closed the scrapbook and hugged it closely. It was a part of her mother she had never known, and it made her feel closer than ever. Suddenly she didn't feel bitter about doing this job. She wondered what other treasures she might find.

"Kitchen" was written on the next several boxes. Sherry had already collected some special things from her mother's kitchen and hadn't planned to go through these remaining trifles. Yet she couldn't resist opening every box...just in case. Slowly and carefully Sherry cut the tape and peered inside. She picked up potholders stained from years of baking and fingered flatware scuffed dull with use.

"No," Sherry told herself firmly as she felt her resolve waver. "I can't keep everything. Where would I put it all?" She re-taped the box and set it aside.

The next box was labeled "dish towels and table linens." *Good, this one should be easy.* But wrapped in one of the towels was the old recipe box her mother had relied on. *How did I miss this earlier?* Reverently she lifted the lid and flipped through the cards, recognizing casseroles and desserts that had been in their family for generations. Sherry smiled when she thought of all the special times she had shared with her mother, preparing meals. Her fingers lingered on the recipe box as she placed it on the growing pile of things she planned to keep.

As she pored through more containers, she lost track of time. Not until she heard the familiar chime of her cell phone did she notice that the sun was descending on the horizon. Laying down an armful of dresses, Sherry reached for her phone. "Hey, Joe," she said, recognizing their home number on the caller ID.

"Hi, sweetie. How's it going over there?"

Sherry blew stray hairs off her forehead as she surveyed the room and sighed. She hadn't even gone through half of the boxes. "Uh...slower than I thought, but OK."

"Are you sure you don't want me to help you?"

"No, no. I'm fine. This way I can go at my own pace." She didn't want an audience as she agonized over things like whether to keep her mother's ragged housecoat, or as she carefully preserved things that seemed silly, like the wrinkled grocery list in her mother's scribbly handwriting.

"Well, call me when you want me to pick up the stuff for the estate sale."

"Sounds good. I'll work a little longer before I call it a day."

Sherry closed her cell phone and turned back toward the pile of clothes she'd set aside. But as she scanned the piles she had yet to sort, fatigue settled in from all the tension and emotion. Strangely, though, she also felt lighter. The knot of anger that had clogged her heart for so long had dissolved.

She ran her hand affectionately over the nearest box. "For another day, Mom," she said softly. "We've accomplished enough for today."

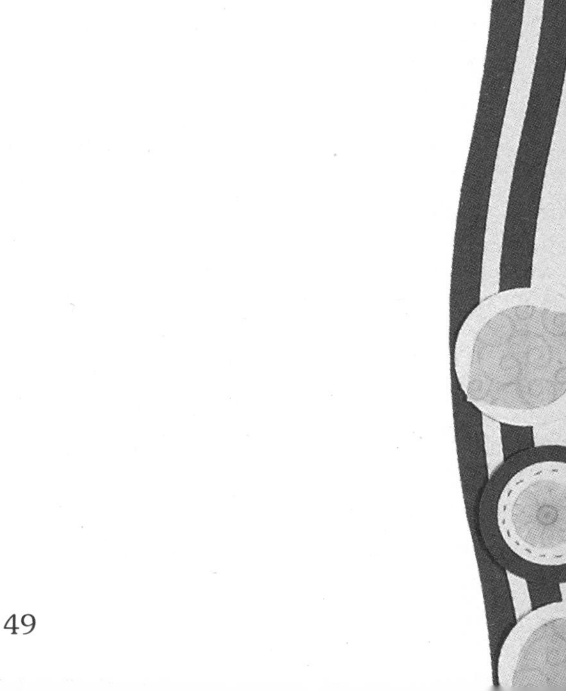

hugs

前 行

雪莉站在一排相同的门前，叹了口气。橘黄色的油漆从仓库的墙上剥落下来，大大小小，散落一地。“真是一个破落、令人沮丧的地方！”她喃喃自语道。

其实并不是这个让她心烦。她计划让自己被足够多的高楼大厦所包围，以来勾勒自己的环境。雪莉手握钥匙，打开了挂锁，猛地一拉门把手，然后就在等待灰色的金属嵌板卷起来流走。

一大早的时候，阳光迅速撒进了那个小房间，将阴影投在了后墙上。雪莉在一大堆堆得几乎到了天花板那么高的箱子中找了半天，然后对如何攻克手边的任务改变了想法。好事情是：妈妈只有一套有两间卧室的双层公寓。她的妈妈经常告诫她，她试图一次应付太多的事情，但是这次，她决心完成这个令人不快的任务。

她的妈妈因大脑动脉瘤突然辞世，这让雪莉大为震惊，感情停滞，就这样将近一年过去了。妈妈向来是她最好的朋友，她的离开给雪莉的生活带来了巨大的空洞。那时候，她几乎不能准备葬礼，整理妈妈的遗物就更别提了。她唯一的兄弟本，住在海外，只能回家来参加葬礼。而她的丈夫乔则建议把她妈妈的遗物存放起来，直到她为这一切做好准备。

雪莉告诉自己，已经做好了充分的准备。她竭力让自己从震惊中走出来继续前进，可在母亲死后她立刻又否定了自己，尽管还是甩不掉内心的愤怒。有些时候气愤得甚至连甩掉愤怒的劲儿都使不出来。她感到自己受骗了——妈妈其实才64岁而已。她那理智的头脑明白，对于发生的一切，她无能为力去预计或阻止，但她仍然对自己没有更多地关注妈妈的身体健康感到恼火。即使她知道那些都无济于事，但她对妈妈的离开还是感到气愤；她对兄弟在妈妈去世之后不能立刻赶回来感到气愤，这是她最需要他的时候。今天在独自处理这些后事时，她——再次——无能为力，对此她感到异常愤怒。她生那些自己所爱的人的气，这也令她气愤。有些时候，就像是只有负罪感让她体会自己日益膨胀的痛苦。

但是，就在她面对像整理妈妈的遗物这样的任务束手无策时，一阵全新的怨恨冲走了一切，甚至是那种负罪感，并带来了新鲜的愤怒。“好吧！”她想到，“我就要来战胜它！”

撂起衣袖，雪莉开始推开和放倒那些标注着“书”“税收纪录”和“衣服”的盒子，甚至连开都没开。一阵莫名的兴奋让她活力四射了差不多半个小时。之后，她的动作缓和了一点儿，对标有“瓷器”和“装饰品”的盒子更加小心，盯着里面好一会儿，时间长得足够她把想留下来作纪念的任何物品拽出来，但是想要让她的情绪再次达到最佳状态，时间还不够长。

下一个盒子是“园艺用品”。妈妈生前热爱园艺，并且总是有用不完的种子、指导手册和工具。也许她应该保留这些。然而她无法看着它们。她把这个盒子加到了最新的“保留”一堆里。

一个没有标记的盒子吸引了雪莉的注意力。好吧，或许又是一堆乱七八糟的杂物而已。她透过捆绑的带子扫了几眼——一些古老的钩针和线。妈妈尝试过作编织手工，可从没有真正开始过。雪莉准备把它归到捐赠的一堆物品里，但把它提起来的时候，它的重量似乎不仅仅是一捆纱线和基本指导手册。奇怪呢。她又放下盒子，在里面仔细翻找。

底部有一个硬硬的东西，拽出来一看是本她从来没见过的巨大的黑皮书。注意到它那破旧的皮革封面时，她的动作缓和下来。她小心翼翼地打开书，发觉这一定是妈妈儿时的剪贴簿。雪莉翻看着每一页上自己从未看过的照片，倒吸一口气。她打开了一张老剪报，上面报道说妈妈赢得了郡里举办的嘉年华选美第一名。还有一张演示的是8年级的报告卡，上面写着“卓越”。她无法读下去——眼泪已经模糊了视线。

“啊……我想我是挺过来了，”雪莉一边飞快地用袖子抹掉眼泪，一边嘴里这么嘟囔着。但是没有用。她都还没来得及翻到下一页，眼泪又流淌下来。几个月来，她第一次在她自我保护般的愤怒盔甲中感到一丝裂痕。她在地上腾出点空儿端着书坐下来。

接下来的一个小时里，雪莉慢慢翻完了这本书，细细品味妈妈的每一个瞬间。她用手指头指着这些古老的照片边缘，哈哈大笑。这是一张妈妈十几岁时的照片，戴着一顶宽大的、傻乎乎的帽子，戏剧化地对着相机撇着嘴巴。它巧妙地捕捉了妈妈过去常有的调皮。

雪莉合上本子，抱得紧紧的。这是她所不知道的妈妈的另一面，让她觉得异常亲近。突然，她做这项工作一点儿也不觉得痛苦了。她想知道还能找到些别的什么珍宝。

“厨房”二字写在下面几个盒子上面。雪莉已经从妈妈的厨房里收集了一些特别的物品，所以不准备检查剩下的这些了。但还是抗拒不了打开每个盒子一探究竟的欲望……为了以防万一。雪莉慢慢地、仔细地割断带子朝里看。她取出多年前因为烘烤而痕迹斑斑的防烫套垫，还有长期使用而磨损的扁平餐具。

“不。”感觉自己的决心动摇时，雪莉坚定地告诉自己，“我不能什么都留着。哪有地方放呢？”于是她重新打了包扔到一边。

接下来的盒子上标记着“擦碗巾和桌布”。好啊，这个很容易处理。但是其中一个包裹里存放着妈妈的做菜小窍门。是不是先前错过了？她毕恭毕敬地提起盖子，快速翻阅着那些卡片，意识到原来很久之前，沙锅菜和饭后甜点就在家族中扎根。当她想到和妈妈共同准备饭菜时候的特殊时光，雪莉会心地笑了。她把小菜谱放在一堆准备保留的物品上，然后手指在上面划来划去。

在她仔细翻看那些容器时，时间悄悄溜走。直到听到熟悉的手机铃声响起，她才意识到太阳已经落到地平线上了。放下一大捧裙子，雪莉抓起手机，看到是家里的号码，她说："嗨，乔！"

"嗨，亲爱的。事情进展得如何？"

雪莉吹了吹额头上的散发，环顾了屋子四周，叹了口气。她甚至连一半箱子都还没处理完。"呃，比想象中的慢，但还算过得去。"

"你肯定不需要我帮忙吗？"

"不，不，我能行。这样我可以控制自己的进度。"她不需要一个观众，在一旁看着她为是否保留妈妈的旧家居服而苦恼，或是他如何小心翼翼地保留下看似傻兮兮的东西，比如妈妈用潦草的笔迹写下的揉得皱巴巴的杂货表。

"好吧，要我来收拾放到estate sale（注：欧美一些孤寡老人死后，由专业公司负责将遗留的房产及财物进行公开甩卖）上的东西时，给我电话。"

“听起来不错。再干一会儿我就收工了。”

雪莉挂上电话，重新回来整理刚才堆到一边的衣服。但当她扫视了一下没有分类的物品时，疲倦从紧张和阴郁的情绪中迸发出来。奇怪的是，尽管如此，她却觉得轻松多了。长久以来积压在心里让她气愤的症结终于解开了。

她温柔地抚摸着身边的盒子。“改天吧，妈妈。我们今天做得够多了。”

Chapter 3

Providing Support

3

给予支持

I've been with you from the beginning, forming you in your mother's womb. No matter where you go or what circumstances you face, you can trust Me to guide you. My right hand will support you. I'll provide for all of your needs according to My unlimited riches in glory.

Supporting you,
Your Ever-Present God

—from Psalm 139:9–13; Philippians 4:19

我必从开始就惠顾你，在你母亲的腹中就庇佑你。无论你去向何方，面对何景，我都必将指引你。我的右手将扶持你。我必以我荣耀的丰富，使你一切所需用的都充足。

主持你，
你无所不在的神

——《诗篇》139：9–13；
《腓利比书》4：19

Memories

Memories

Anyone who loves to scrapbook knows how much more fun it is to do it with friends. In fact, anything done with others is more fun. Whether it's cooking, cleaning, or doing yard work, working alongside others makes the task more enjoyable, and the time seems to fly.

Scrapbooking is an enjoyable hobby; more importantly it's an invaluable tradition that preserves the unique stories of how you live, who you love, and what you value. It does take some time though. Organizing photos, creating page layouts, and journaling all require effort and time. Many people don't scrapbook because it takes so much time. That's why it's so good to get together with friends to

Memories

inspirational message

work on your albums. When you join with others, you're more likely to make it a point to set aside time to work on your photos. Friends encourage each other, inspire each other, and keep each other moving forward when it's easier to do something else instead.

Besides, it's so much fun to look at each other's pictures and hear the stories behind them. You know how much you owe your friends for sharing their great new ideas and materials to help make your pages unique and beautiful. Not to mention that you can get lots of great advice on parenting, marriage, and life in general in the process. Now, that's a support group!

喜欢剪贴簿的人都知道，和朋友们一起做这件事真的是太有趣了。事实上，只要是有他人参与的事情都是比较有意思的。无论是烹饪、清洁，或是在院子里劳动，和他人一起工作都会让这些事情更有乐趣，并且你会感觉到时间飞逝而过。

制作剪贴簿是一个可以让人身心愉悦的爱好，更为重要的是，它是一项意义非凡的传统，这个传统可以让你记下身边独一无二的故事、无法代替的爱情，你与众不同的价值，尽管会花去你一些时间。收集照片，设计版面，记录下每天发生的事情，这些都需要不懈的努力和时间。许多人不愿意制作剪贴簿，因为它的确要花费太多的时间。

那也

是为什么和朋友们一起为你的剪贴簿工作是一件美差。当你和朋友们一起为此工作时，更有可能使他们特别留出时间来共同剪贴你的照片这件事情成真。朋友间的相互鼓励，相互启发，不断让对方前行，这样反而可以更轻松地做一些事情。

除此之外，大家互相看着彼此的照片，听着照片背后的故事，这真的是太有意思了。你知道吗？你应该感激你的朋友们和你共享他们很棒的新想法和新素材，这些让剪贴簿的页面变得独一无二、且美丽无边。不必提及你获得的有关的孩子的养育，婚姻生活，日常生活中太多宝贵的建议。现在，他们是你强有力的后盾。

Every true friend

is a glimpse of god.

Lucy Larcom

How could she dare admit
even to herself—much less
anyone else—that she
resented the very people and
things she loved so much?

Crop Night

Betsy sighed wearily as she put her Cavalier in park and turned off the ignition. She leaned back against the headrest and closed her eyes for one sweet moment of peace, solitude, and rest. She willed her body to move—Kimberly and Donna were waiting for her, and she was already late—but her body wouldn't obey. She was so tired, and she had already missed nearly an hour. Maybe no one would notice if she just curled up on the seat and napped.

She lifted her head and opened her eyes wide, battling their inclination to close. She knew if she didn't move now, she really would fall asleep. For the first time, she recognized that her weariness was tinged with resentment—resentment of her friends for expecting her to come to something as trivial as a scrapbook night when she had so many more important things to do; resentment of her husband for encouraging—no, insisting—that it would be good for her to come tonight; resentment of all the impossible expectations life had placed on her shoulders; even resentment at little Addison for needing so much and taking so much of her mother's time and energy. But how could she dare admit even to herself—much less anyone else—that she resented the very people and things she loved so much?

She sighed again and gathered up her mountains of scrapbooks and supplies. She might as well get it over with. At least it would be one more thing she could cross off her list—if she could even find her list. She tried to at least look happy as she carefully made her way to the door.

Betsy didn't want to put down the stack of scrapbooks in her arms, so she pressed the doorbell with her elbow. As she did, a heavy canvas bag slipped from her shoulder. She shifted her weight to the other side, unwittingly causing the stuffed bag on her other shoulder to slip down to rest in the crook of her arm, almost causing her to drop the scrapbooks.

Not a moment too soon, her friend Kimberly came to the door.

"Help!" Betsy pleaded, offering the pile of books to her hostess.

With a quick hand, Kimberly grabbed the load and held an arm out to steady Betsy. "Oh, there you are. We were getting concerned. Now why didn't you just make two trips?"

Hoisting each bag onto its respective shoulder, she smiled guiltily. "I didn't think I had enough energy for another trip," Betsy confessed. "Besides, I'm Super Mom. I can handle a load bigger than that while bathing the baby and cooking dinner." She laughed as she moved inside the house. "Sorry I'm late."

Kimberly followed, kicking the door closed behind her. "No problem. Donna is already set up in the kitchen," Kimberly said, nodding toward their destination.

"Hi, Betsy." Donna greeted her friend and took one of the bags from her shoulder.

Betsy slumped into the chair reserved for her. "Hey," she sighed as if it were the first time she'd sat down all day.

"Having one of those days, huh?" Donna sounded empathetic.

Raising her eyebrows, Betsy forced a smile. "Most definitely one of those days. I left a pile of dishes in the sink, and the sofa was piled high with laundry to be folded. Addison has an ear infection, so she wanted me to hold her all day long. I couldn't get anything done! "

"Oh, Betsy! " Kimberly chided. "It sounds like you desperately need a break! "

Propping her elbows on the table, Betsy rested

her chin in her hands. "That's what Chad said too. I wasn't going to come, but he practically threw me out the door. He said I was way too stressed and I needed a time-out. I didn't even know mommies could be sent to time-out!"

Donna squeezed Betsy's shoulders. "Well, I think all mommies should get more time-outs. I don't know how many times I've had to beg Tom to take the kids just so I can bathe in peace. Most daddies I know don't do sick babies. You're fortunate to have a husband who actually encourages you to go."

Kimberly nodded in agreement, and Betsy realized they were right. She halfheartedly retrieved her paper cutter. "Well, I might as well try to get something accomplished tonight. It's already almost nine o'clock. The way my day has gone, I'll be lucky if I finish anything."

"I haven't gotten much done in the past hour," Donna commiserated. "I'm so far behind!"

Pulling out a binder of stickers, Betsy agreed.

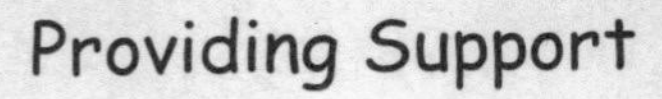

"I'm glad I'm not the only one behind! Addison is already five months old, and I have ten rolls of pictures I've got to do something with. I feel so overwhelmed, I hardly feel like trying to catch up."

Kimberly encouraged her friends. "Just do a little. Even if you get one page done, you'll feel good about it. Every bit helps." She held up a two-page spread featuring photos from her family vacation at Disney World. "How does this look?"

Donna looked up from her pile of pictures. "Too cute! You guys really had a fun time, didn't you?"

The three friends fell comfortably into their routine of cropping. For a moment they worked quietly, each focused on her own project. Betsy yawned loudly, breaking the silence. "I'm so tired! I really should be in bed. Addison still isn't sleeping through the night, and it's wearing me out!"

"Here, have a little caffeine," Kimberly said, handing her a soda and a chocolate-chip cookie. "It works for me, but then again, I get a pretty good night's sleep. Zachary still comes into our bed in the middle of the night, but at least he's tricky enough to sneak in and not make a sound. I don't wake up until his foot slaps me in the face! "

Donna groaned, recalling her own experience. "Laney didn't sleep through the night till she was eighteen months old! It was miserable. Sometimes I still wake up at 2 a.m. and think I hear my baby's cry—and she's eight! "

The friends laughed with humor and empathy.

Kimberly stifled her laugh, placing a finger to her lips. "Shh, or we'll wake up my kids! I certainly don't want to fight getting them back to bed."

They resumed their work, suppressing infectious giggles. Once again the room was filled with the familiar sounds of scissor clipping and paper punching. It wasn't long before each of them had something to show from the night's work.

Kimberly stood up to refill her drink. "That looks great! " she said, looking over Donna's shoulder.

"Let me see! " Betsy requested, holding up her own completed page of Addison's first bath.

Donna held up her page, and they exchanged compliments.

With keen eyes Betsy examined her friend's technique. Donna had mounted her sister's wedding photo on vellum. "I love that idea. I need to try it on Addison's baby scrapbook.

"Have I shown you the pictures from Addison's dedication at church? The vellum will be perfect for what I'm thinking of doing with that page."

Kimberly picked up a picture of Addison in her christening gown and passed it to Donna. "She's such a pretty baby," Donna mused.

The next photo was of Betsy's family standing before the entire congregation, praying. "That was one of the first times I'd seen you," Kimberly remembered. "I thought Addison was one of the most beautiful babies I'd ever seen, and I just had to tell you after the service."

Betsy smiled. "We'd joined the church only a few months before. It was so thoughtful of you to introduce yourself and pay such a sweet compliment to Addison. If you hadn't, we might never have become such good friends."

"Oh, you only liked me because I said you had a cute baby," Kimberly replied mischievously.

"Hey, anyone who says my baby is beautiful is my new best friend," Betsy joked. The three burst into giggles once more, this time remembering the sleeping children. "Seriously though. I was new to the church and didn't know very many people. You invited me to your house and got me working on my first album."

"I could tell you'd be a good scrapbooker," Kimberly responded with a wink.

Just then the grandfather clock chimed midnight, time to quit.

"Is it twelve o'clock already?" Betsy looked at her watch. She could hardly believe it was so late. She felt awake and rejuvenated—like she could keep right on working.

Donna closed her books and zipped up her scrapbook tote. "You look a lot better," she told Betsy. "Now aren't you glad you came?"

"Yes! " Betsy replied exuberantly. "Not only did I complete eight pages, I *do* feel much better."

As she loaded up her supplies, she realized that along with the weariness, the resentment was also gone. Working with the photos and her friends had reminded her that what sometimes felt like burdens were actually blessings. She had a wonderful, caring husband. Her baby was beautiful, precious, and whole. And she had been blessed with friends who understood what she was going through and offered the encouragement of perspective. Those things were worth remembering. She resolved to cherish this revelation in the scrapbook of her heart.

收获之夜

贝特西疲倦地叹了一口气，将雪佛兰“骑士”停入停车场，熄灭引擎。她向后斜靠在一个枕头上，闭上眼睛以享受片刻的平静、安宁和休憩。她希望自己的身体可以移动——金伯利和唐娜正在等候她，她已经迟到了——但是她的身体一点儿也不听话。她真的是太累了，差不多迟到快一个小时了。如果她蜷缩在坐椅上打个小盹，或许谁也不会注意到。

她抬起头，睁大眼睛，和睡意作斗争。她知道如果她现在不动弹，她真的会立刻就睡着。生平第一次，她意识到自己的疲倦还因为些许的愤懑之情——愤懑是因为她的朋友们期待她的到来，晚上一起做制作剪贴簿这样微不足道的小事，愤懑是因为她的丈夫的鼓励——不，怂恿——他认为今晚的参与对她来说意义非凡；愤懑是因为年幼的阿狄森花费她太多时间和精力去照顾。但是她

怎么敢对自己承认——更别说其他人了——她厌烦的是自己深深爱着对自己来说特别的人和事?

她又叹了口气，将堆得像山一样的剪贴簿和平时的素材收集起来。她最好一劳永逸。至少她可以从自己的日程表上画去这件多余的事情——如果她恰好能够找到自己的日程表的话。她小心翼翼地向门前走去,并且努力让自己至少看起来很开心。

贝特西不想将怀中的一大摞剪贴簿放下，因此她用胳膊肘按响了门铃。当她正在按门铃时,一个很沉的帆布包从她肩头滑落。她将自己的重心移向另外一边,这个不明智的举动使得背在另外一边被塞得满满的包滑落下来，滑到了她的臂弯处,几乎让她将剪贴簿散落到了地上。

过了好一会儿,她的朋友金伯利才来开门。

“帮帮忙!”贝特西边恳求,边把怀中的剪贴簿交给女主人。

眼疾手快,金伯利抢过沉甸甸的一摞剪贴簿,一边伸出手臂扶住贝特西,“噢,你在这儿,大家刚刚一直惦记你。你为什么不做两次旅行呢?”

她将包分别往两个肩膀上提了提,内疚地微笑着。“我认为我没有精力再来一次,”贝特西坦白地说。“除此之外,我是个超级妈咪，我可以在为宝宝洗澡和做饭时搬运很重的东西。”她大笑着,走进屋子里。“对不起,我迟到了。”

金伯利跟着进了屋，踢了一脚门，门在她身后关上。“没问题，唐娜已经在厨房忙活了，”金伯利说，扬了扬下巴示意他俩的目的地。

“嗨，贝特西。”唐娜和朋友问了声好，将一个包从她肩膀上取了下来。

贝特西半躺在为她预留的椅子上。“嗨！”她叹了口气，仿佛一整天她第一次坐下来。

“这几天一直在忙吗？”唐娜体贴地说。

扬了扬眉毛，贝特西挤出一个微笑。“一直在忙。我放下一叠盘子在水槽里，沙发堆得高高的，有很多要叠的衣服，艾迪有耳疾，因此她需要我整天抱着她。我什么事都不能做了！”

“噢，贝特西！”金伯利轻斥。“看来你急切地需要休息一阵子！”

贝特西的胳膊支着桌子，用手托着脸颊。“查德也这么说。其实我本来不想来的，但是他几乎是将我扔出了门。他说我是压力太大了，需要休息。我甚至都不知道妈妈们也能有空休息。”

唐娜紧握住贝特西的肩膀。“好啦，我认为所有的妈妈都应该有更多的休息。我不知道我曾经多少次请求汤姆照看好孩子，以便我可以平静地洗一次澡。据我所知，大多数爸爸们都不愿照顾生病的孩子。你真幸运有这样的先生，他居然鼓励你出门。”

金伯利点头表示赞同，贝特西意识到他们是对的。她冷冷地取回她的切纸机。“好啦，今晚我或许该尽力获得一些成就感。都已经快9点了。我的一天就这样流逝了，如果我做完了一些事情我会觉得很幸运。”

“时间如流水。”唐娜同情地说。“我已经落后太多了！”

贝特西一边取出黏合剂贴纸，一边表示同意。“我真开心我不是唯一落后的人！艾迪已经5个月大了，我已经有10卷照片去做剪贴簿了。我觉得很沮丧，我觉得我肯定赶不上大家了。”

金伯利鼓励她的朋友们。“再多做一些。即使你只完成了一页，你也会感觉非常棒。每完成一点都会让你觉得成就非凡。”她举起占两个版面的有特色的照片，这些是全家去迪斯尼乐园度假时拍的。“这看起来如何？”

唐娜从一堆堆的照片中抬起头。“太可爱了！小伙子你的的确确没有虚度时光，难道不是么？”

三个朋友感觉开心极了，因为他们一直以来的努力得到了回报。有那么一阵子他们安安静静地工作着。每个人都专注于自己的项目。贝特西大声地打了一个呵欠，打破了片刻的沉寂。“我太累了！我真该上床去休息一下。艾迪仍旧整夜不睡觉，这让我筋疲力尽！”

“给你，来点提神的东西。”金伯利边说边递给了她一罐汽水和一片巧克力口味的曲奇。“这对我来说很有效，但我还是睡了个好觉。扎克瑞在半夜才上床睡觉，但至少他是轻手轻脚地溜进卧室，没有弄出丝毫的声响。直到他的脚碰到了我的脸，我才醒。”

唐娜叹了一口气，她想起自己的经历。“兰妮在18个月之前通宵不睡觉！那段时间生活真的是太糟糕了，有时候凌晨 2点我还睡不着，我总觉得自己听到了宝宝的哭声——现在她都8岁了！”

朋友们充满善意，会心地笑做一团。

金伯利竭力忍住笑声，将一个指头压在嘴唇上。“嘘，否则我们会吵醒孩子们！我确定我不想再奋力和他们作斗争，为的是把他们弄回床上睡觉。”

他们又继续开始工作，抑制住大家互相感染的咯咯的笑声。房间里再次满是熟悉的剪刀裁纸和给纸打孔的声音。不久，他们每个人都有一些夜晚可展示的成绩。

金伯利站起身，给自己加满水。“看起来棒极了！”她说，她从唐娜肩膀上方看着唐娜的杰作。

“让我看看！”贝特西提出请求，边举起自己已经完成的艾迪第一次洗澡的页面。

唐娜举起自己的页面，她们互相称赞着对方。

贝特西用敏锐的目光审视着好友的制作技术。唐娜将自己姐姐的照片也放入精制羔皮纸上。“我喜欢这个点子。我该在艾迪婴儿时的相册上试试看。”

“我给你们看艾迪在教堂献辞的照片了吗？精制羔皮纸是我能考虑到的用在那一面上的最棒的选择。”

金伯利挑了一张艾迪穿洗礼的袍子的照片，递给了唐娜。“她真是个漂亮的孩子。”唐娜若有所思地凝望着照片说。

接下来的一张照片是贝特西全家站在全部的会众之前祈祷。“那是我第一次看到你。”金伯利回忆道。“当时我认为，艾迪是我见过的最漂亮的孩子，我本想在礼拜后告诉你的。”

贝特西微笑着。“我们是在几个月前加入教会的。你真的很有思想，不仅向大家介绍了你自己，还给予了艾迪甜美的赞美。如果你没有这么做，我们或许永远也不会成为这么好的朋友。”

“噢，你喜欢我仅仅是因为我说你有个可爱的宝宝。”金伯利调皮地回答。

“嗨，无论是谁说我的孩子漂亮，都是我最好的朋友。”贝特西开玩笑地说。三个好朋友再次迸发出咯咯的笑声，这次她们想起还有正在睡觉的孩子们。“仔细想想，以前我对礼拜并不熟悉并且认识的人也不多。你邀请我去你家并且让我成功制作了我的第一本相册。”

“我可以说你会是个很棒的家庭相册制作者。”金伯利眨了眨眼睛回答。

这时落地大座钟敲响了午夜的钟声，是大家分别的时间了。

“都已经12点了？”贝特西看了看手表。她无法确信时间都这么晚了。她感觉一点睡意也没有，并且精力充沛——仿佛她可以不停地做剪贴簿。

唐娜合上自己的一本本剪贴簿，拉上了装剪贴簿手提包的拉链。“你看上去好多了，”她对贝特西说。“难道你没觉得你不虚此行么？”

“当然！”贝特西兴高采烈地回答。“我不仅仅是完成了8页的工作量，而且我真的感觉舒服多了。”

当她背起行囊，除了感觉疲倦，自己的愤懑不平早已烟消云散。和朋友们一起整理照片，让她回想起有时生活的重担实际上是上帝的祝福。她有位无可挑剔，对她宠爱有加的先生。她心爱的宝宝漂亮又健康。她的朋友们总是祝福她，她们知道她该走出何种困境，并且不停给她鼓励，让她对未来充满希望。那些都是值得回味一生的，她决意珍惜这从剪贴簿中获得的意想不到的心灵发现。

Chapter 4

Investing Yourself

4 舍得投入

你不要只顾自己的事，也要顾及别人的事。你的善行将为我增添荣誉，而我将切实地实现我的职责，就从你开始。
关注你的，
体恤你的神
——《腓利比书》2:4；
《彼得前书》2:12；
《腓利比书》1:6

Life is about more than just you. Make a positive investment by looking out for the interests of others. Live your life so that your good deeds give credit to me, and know that I'll faithfully complete the good work I've started in you.

Investing in you,
Your Gracious God

—*from Philippians 2:4; Peter 2:12; Philippians 1:6*

Doesn't it feel good when you've completed a scrapbook page? After you've placed that final sticker or completed the caption beside the last photo, it's so nice to inspect and appreciate your work.

Seeing that special event displayed, embellished just the way you like, and being able to show it to others, brings a sense of accomplishment. Even if you didn't spend a lot of time making the page or adding a lot of extra detail, it's satisfying just to see the photos in a book instead of stuffed in a box under a bed somewhere.

Plenty of scrapbookers don't claim to be creative. But with all the die cuts, stickers, and papers available, anybody can make a great-looking scrapbook page just

inspirational message

by putting all the pieces together and adding their own personal stories. No matter what your level of skill or effort in creating scrapbook pages, you can call it a job well done because it's your special touch—you've invested a part of yourself.

It's rewarding to look at your work and say, I did that! And isn't it fun to sit back and listen to the *oohs and ahhs* of approval from friends and family as they compliment you on your latest masterpieces?

Don't be afraid to invest yourself and your time in a scrapbook, and by doing so, in others. Not only are you creating one-of-a-kind artwork for your family to enjoy, you're preserving memories for yourself and for generations to come.

完成了剪贴簿的一个页面时感觉是不是特别好？在你涂上最后一下胶水，完成最后一张照片旁边的说明文字之后，鉴赏你的成果会感觉很舒服。

看见用喜欢的风格排版、修饰出来的一个有特殊意义的事件，展示在别人面前，是一件很有成就感的事。即使你没有花费特别多的时间在制作页面和添加细节上，看到照片集结成册也比看到它们被塞在床底下的某个箱子里令人满意。

好多剪贴爱好者本身不是很有创意。但是如果手边有各种式样的花边、粘胶和纸张，谁都可以只是通过把所有材料组织在一起并加上他们自己的故事，制作出赏心悦目的剪贴簿。

不管你的水平如何，页面创作中投入了几成努力，你都可以说它是一件好作品，因为那是你自己的——你将自己已经投入其中。

看着自己的成果，你说道“是我做的!”会很有成就感。而且，听着朋友和家人因为你的这份最新杰作而说出的褒奖之词，很有趣吧?

不要舍不得把自己的精力和时间投入剪贴簿中，或者是同样地投入给其他人、其他事。你不仅为你的家人创造了一件艺术品，你还为自己和后代留下了一份记忆。

The noblest question
in the world is,
what good may I do in it?
Benjamin Franklin

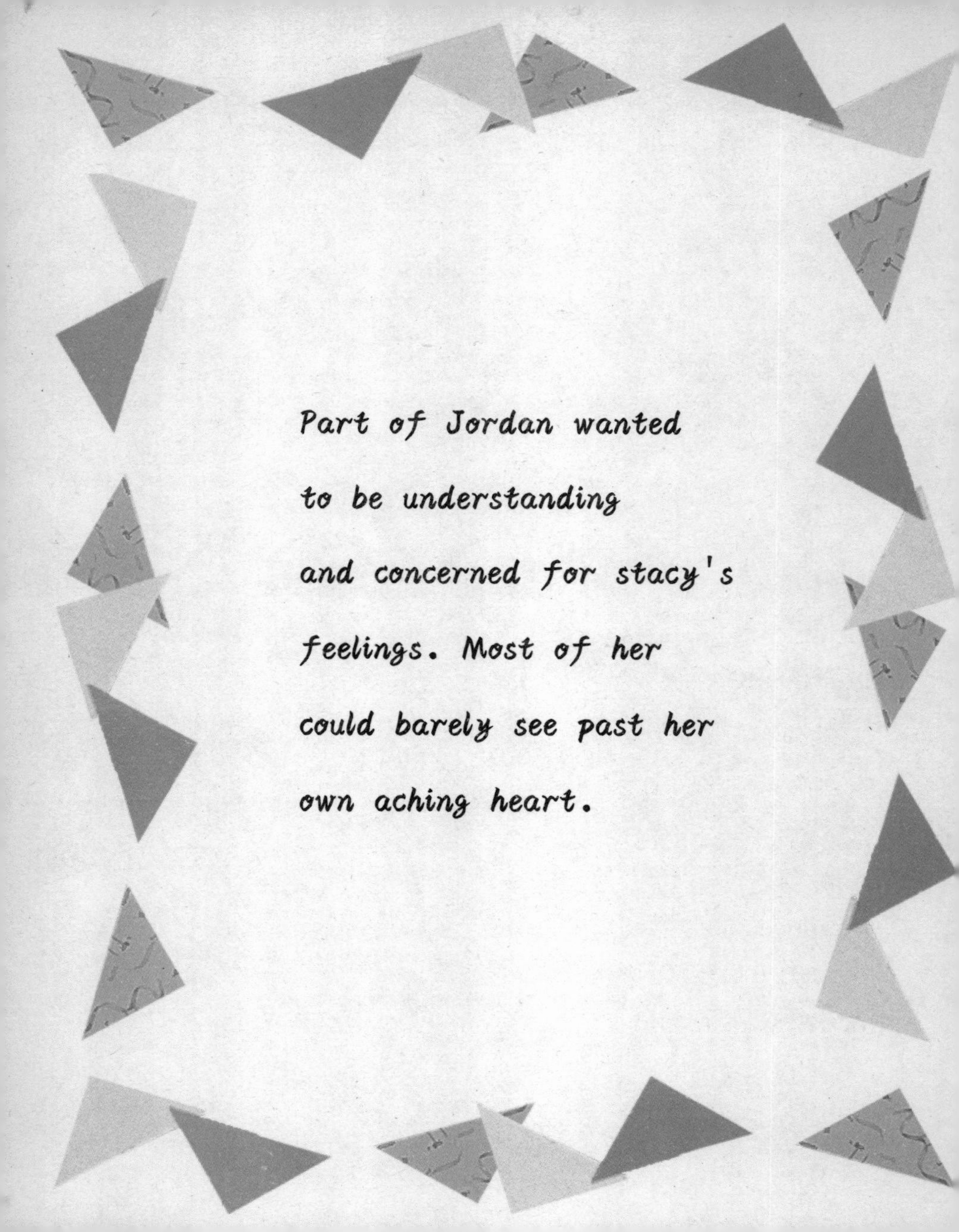

Part of Jordan wanted
to be understanding
and concerned for stacy's
feelings. Most of her
could barely see past her
own aching heart.

Torn

Jordan hugged her algebra book tightly to her chest like a shield against further attack. She was in such a hurry to leave school that she didn't even take time to put it in her backpack. She didn't want to meet anyone's eyes and have to force a smile or risk someone noticing she was upset, so she hung her head low and fought her shoulders' natural inclination to slump dejectedly. Her eyes never left the dirty, tiled floor. It was a wonder she made it through the hall-ways unharmed. Mechanically she made her way to the parking lot.

Once outside, Jordan scanned the cars lined up in the pick-up area. Desperately she searched for her mother's silver minivan and then hastily fled toward it.

"Hi, Jordan! " her mother greeted her cheerfully when she opened the door.

"Hi, Mom," Jordan said quietly, dumping her backpack on the floor and sliding quickly into the seat. She closed the door and buckled her seatbelt, sinking as low as she could into the safety and protective cover of the seat.

Out of the corner of her eye, she could tell that her mom was looking at her. Could she tell? Curious, she turned to meet her mother's eyes. That one glance was all it took. Her mother's look of concern broke the defensive wall she'd carefully built up. Jordan could hold back no longer. Tears spilled from her eyes.

"Oh, sweetheart, what's the matter?" her mom prodded gently.

"This girl ... "Jordan sniffed and had trouble continuing."She was really mean to me today."

"Tell me what happened."

"Her name is Stacy. I don't know why she doesn't like me. I've never done anything to her! " Jordan wiped the tears away with the back of her hand in an attempt to control their flow. In broken sentences between sobs, she recounted the dreadful event. "She knocked into me on purpose. I dropped all my stuff...her friends were laughing..."

"I'm so sorry, baby." Jordan felt her mom's hand on her leg, first patting soothingly, then adding a reassuring squeeze.

"That's not all," Jordan persisted, unzipping her backpack. "Stacy picked up my folder and tore it. She said it was an accident, but she and her friends walked away laughing."

She pulled out the ruined folder. Jordan had created a miniature scrapbook page on the front. She'd meticulously placed flower and heart stickers around the perimeter as a border, and in the center she'd mounted a picture of her dog, Coco. Seeing the torn photo brought fresh tears.

Jordan didn't think of herself as thin-skinned. In

fact, she had always been good at fending off jokes thrown her way. While she handled teasing with grace, this was one prank that had cut straight to the heart. She wasn't good at sports or cheer-leading like many of her peers, but she'd discovered a creative ability through her scrapbooks. She'd even joined the yearbook committee to pursue her talent further. It had been exciting to finally find something she could do really well.

The car came to a halt, and Jordan was surprised to realize they were already home. Her mom turned off the ignition, and for a moment they sat in silence. When her mom did speak, her voice was calm and deliberate. "We don't know why Stacy did what she did today. We don't know what life is like at her house. It may be that she hurts others because she's hurting too. We just don't know."

Jordan met her mother's eyes and felt sustained as she continued. "I do know that God tells us to pray for our enemies. Why don't we say a prayer for Stacy? Let's also pray that you'll know what to do if something like this ever happens again."

Part of Jordan wanted to be understanding, and concerned for Stacy's feelings. Most of her could barely see past her own aching heart. Dutifully Jordan bowed her head and prayed for Stacy.

That evening Jordan pulled out her torn folder at her scrapbooking table and surveyed the damage. The folder and border were a complete loss, and the photo of Coco was torn, but maybe she could rescue it by turning the tom edges into a special effect. Although still wounded at such a public and unprovoked attack, she felt a surge of joy and confidence in her ability to creatively turn even the tragedy of a torn photo into something with purpose and beauty. She waited for the inspiration to hit as it always did.

Suddenly she felt the rough outline of an idea starting to form at the edges of her consciousness. The boldness of the idea startled her, and she tried to turn her thoughts in other directions, but she couldn't. The idea clicked. It was the right thing to do.

Her hands started moving quickly, proficiently, to capture her idea on paper before it flew away. She applied stickers and die cuts and her favorite paper designs. With satisfaction and determination, she knew this would be her best work yet.

The next day at school, just after the five-minute warning bell, Jordan spotted Stacy and her crowd. Jordan's heart raced, and she pulled her books to her chest defensively. For a moment she considered ducking into the nearest classroom, but it was too late to turn back. Stacy had spotted her. She pointed at Jordan and said something Jordan couldn't hear that evoked smirks and laughter among the other girls.

With resolve and a boldness that surprised her, Jordan stepped up to face Stacy. She thought perhaps Stacy would tear the new scrapbook page in which she'd invested so much effort and hope, but she pushed the fear aside. The momentary surprise she saw on Stacy's face gave her added courage.

"Hi, Stacy." Jordan managed to smile. "I was

scrapbooking again last night. I want you to see what I made." She thrust her latest work of art into Stacy's hand, then turned and walked resolutely toward her first class. This time she held her head high and felt a spring of confidence and pride. She'd sent the bully a pointed message. However Stacy chose to respond, Jordan felt good that she hadn't let Stacy intimidate her or dictate how she'd act.

But as the day wore on, that confidence was slowly replaced with uncertainty. It was like waiting for the other shoe to drop, wondering if she might suddenly encounter Stacy around each next corner. She almost wished she hadn't done it. What was she thinking?

When the dismissal bell rang that afternoon, Jordan decided she'd better clear out fast, before she had to risk facing Stacy's group alone in the empty halls. She had just opened her locker when someone from behind her slammed it shut again, making her jump. She instantly knew it was Stacy. Being this close to her bully took Jordan's breath away. Last night this had seemed like a good idea, but now she wasn't so sure. She hoped she'd be strong enough to handle a bad reaction from Stacy. She turned with dread to face her, silently praying for Stacy and for strength for herself.

Stacy thrust Jordan's card in her face accusingly. "What's this?" She demanded.

"It's a card," Jordan responded, caught off guard by the simplicity of the question.

Stacy paused before continuing, as if confused. "Did you really make this for me?"

Jordan nodded.

"But why?"

Jordan smiled and pointed to the words written meticulously with fancy flourishes. "Did you read it? It says I want us to be friends."

"I know what it says," Stacy said impatiently. "But how can you mean that? After how I've treated you...after yesterday..."

"I do mean it, Stacy," Jordan assured her. "I don't know what I might have done to annoy or offend you, but I'm sorry. I'd rather be your friend than your enemy. Can we be friends?"

She watched as Stacy fingered the card almost reverently. "It's really pretty—and a lot of work." Suddenly Stacy seemed softer, even a little vulnerable. With growing compassion and understanding, Jordan decided her mom had been right, that sometimes bullies just need to be loved. She was glad she had prayed for Stacy and proud that she'd done the right thing.

"But after what happened yesterday," Stacy mumbled, carefully avoiding meeting Jordan's eyes. "I was so mean to you."

"I forgive you, Stacy," Jordan assured her.

Finally Stacy looked up nervously. "I would like for us to be friends."

Jordan smiled broadly. "That's great! Maybe I could show you my scrapbook stuff sometime?"

"I'd like that," Stacy said, relaxing and smiling for the first time. "Do you want to talk about it during lunch tomorrow? Maybe I could sit with you."

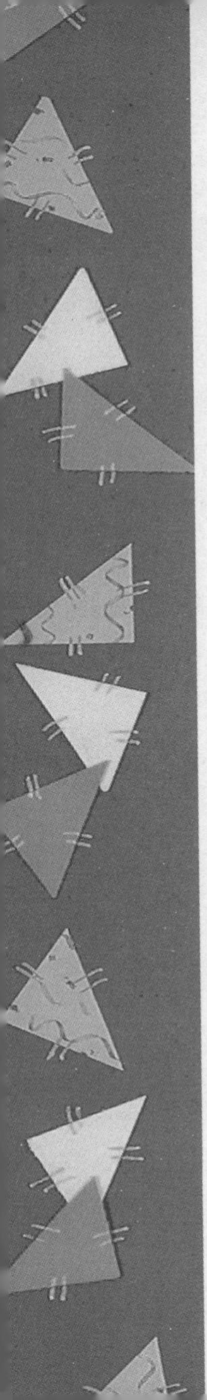

Grinning widely, Jordan nodded. "That would be great!" Suddenly she was aware that the halls had emptied of students. She glanced at her watch. "Yikes, it's getting late. My mom is waiting for me. She'll probably be thinking I got mugged in here or something." She smiled again at Stacy. "I'll see you tomorrow...friend."

Stacy smiled. It was a nice smile, Jordan decided.

Jordan waved goodbye and raced toward the door, hugging her algebra book tightly across her chest and feeling her heart pounding wildly against it. She could hardly contain her excitement. Not only was she using her creative talents to find her own identity, she was using them to encourage others. She could hardly wait to tell her mom.

破 碎

乔丹不想再受到伤害，她把代数课本像盾牌一样紧紧抱在胸前，甚至没有来得及把它放进背包里，就匆忙跑出了学校。她不想面对任何人的目光，也不想去强颜欢笑或是暴露出自己的沮丧，所以她一直低垂着头，双眼死死盯着脚下满是尘土的地砖，强撑着身体，不让它瘫软下去。谢天谢地，乔丹毫发无损地穿过走廊，径直向停车场走去。

一到室外，乔丹的目光便在一排一排汽车中急切地找寻着妈妈的银色迷你车，并飞快地冲了过去。

“嗨，乔丹！”拉开车门时，妈妈热情地和她打招呼。

而她只是平静地说了声“嗨，妈妈”，便卸下背包，迅速坐下。关上车门，系好安全带，小小的身体不断地下沉，像是在向座位寻求安全和庇护。

乔丹用眼角的余光就知道妈妈在看着她。要不要告诉她呢？小心翼翼地，她转头迎向妈妈的目光。可就是这一瞬的四目相对，妈妈慈爱的目光便摧毁了她精心构筑的心理防线。按捺不住的泪水夺眶而出。

“哦，宝贝儿，发生什么事了？”妈妈轻声地问道。

“这女孩……”乔丹抽泣着，声音哽咽。“她今天对我实在是太恶劣了。”

“告诉我，究竟发生了什么事？”

“她叫史黛西，我也不知道为什么她不喜欢我，我从来没有招惹她啊！”乔丹用手背擦掉脸上汩汩流下的眼泪。她用断断续续、夹杂着啜泣的言语，叙说着那可怕的一幕。“她故意朝我撞过来。我手里的东西都掉了……她的朋友们就在一旁嘲笑我……”

“真是难为你了，宝贝！”乔丹感觉到妈妈的手抚慰着她，拍了拍她的腿，给了她一份恢复信心的力量。

“我还没有说完，”乔丹说话间拉开了背包链。“史黛西捡起我的文件夹，撕得粉碎。她说这只是个意外，可是她和朋友们走开时还一直在笑。”

她把破碎的文件夹从书包里拽出来，封皮是乔丹自己创作的一页迷你剪贴画。她曾小心翼翼地用花瓣和心形贴纸镶边，还在中心位置嵌上了她的爱犬科科的照片。看着破碎的照片，她又禁不住流下了眼泪。

乔丹不觉得自己是个脆弱的女孩。实际上，她很善于对别人跟她开的玩笑见招拆招。然而当她用优雅应对恼人的嘲弄时，这个恶作剧真的深深伤了她的心。她并不擅长体育运动或是调动大家的情绪，但是她在剪贴画中发现了自己非凡的创作力。为了让自己的才华得以施展，她还加入了年鉴委员会。终于找到自己所长，这让她兴奋不已。

车子停了下来，乔丹这才意识到已经到家了。妈妈把车子熄了火，两个人沉默着坐了好一会儿。当妈妈开始说话时，她的声音带着平静和深思：“我们不知道她在家里过着怎样的生活。伤害别人很可能是因为她自己也在忍受着伤害。我们只是无从知晓罢了。”

乔丹看到妈妈的眼睛，觉得这眼神中充满了支持和鼓励。妈妈继续说：“我只知道，上帝要我们为我们的敌人也祈祷、祝福。为史黛西祈祷吧，也祈祷你在这种事情再次发生的情况下知道如何应对。”

乔丹想要去关心、理解史黛西的心情，可是仍然隐隐作痛的心让她无法释怀。她还是虔诚地低下了头，为史黛西祷告。

当晚，乔丹拿出破碎的文件夹，铺在自己的剪贴画桌上，细数着伤痕。纸夹和花边已经完全松脱，科科的照片也破了，不过也许还有救，可以通过将碎边拼接在一起，达成一种特殊的效果。虽然在大庭广众之下被无缘无故地伤害，她心中还是涌起了一阵喜悦，因为她将化腐朽为神奇，她满怀信心准备将这悲剧里的碎照片变成唯美的手工。她思索着，像往常一样等待着灵感的迸发。

忽然，意识里出现了一点点粗略的创意，她惊异于自己大胆的想法，想要甩掉这个想法，可她控制不了。这个创意恰当极了。照做就对了。

她的巧手开始迅速地飞舞起来，创意还没来得及飘走，就被她手到擒来。粘胶、剪影和她最爱的花纸图案淋漓尽致地发挥了它们的作用。她坚信，这一定会是她最好的一件作品。

第二天的学校里，预备铃刚刚响过5分钟，乔丹就发现了史黛西和她的小集体。乔丹心跳加速，自卫似的把书紧紧抱在胸前。要不要直接闪进最近的一间教室？她挣扎了好一会儿，可是此时转身已经晚了，史黛西已经看到她了。史黛西手指着乔丹，嘴里说了些什么，乔丹听不到，可是那话却引起了那帮女孩们的轻嘲和讥笑。

乔丹走上前去直面史黛西，这份决心和勇敢令她自己都无法想象。她猜想，史黛西也许会把她倾注了努力和希望的新剪贴画页再次撕掉，可她还是把恐惧抛在了脑后。史黛西的脸上瞬间闪现出的诧异给了乔丹更多的勇气。

“嗨，史黛西！”乔丹强作笑颜，“我昨晚又重新做了一遍剪贴画，我想让你看看我的作品。”她把自己最新的艺术品塞在史黛西的手里，就转身径直走向了第一节课的教室。这次，乔丹高昂着头，心底涌出一阵阵的自信和自豪。她已经向欺凌弱小者发出了信息，而史黛西也选择了回应；她没有被史黛西吓倒，也让她没能重复昨天的行为，这都让乔丹感觉很好。

然而随着时间慢慢过去，自信渐渐地被不确定感所取代。这种情形如同深夜静候楼上本该扔下的另一只鞋子。乔丹总想着会不会突然在某个拐角遇上史黛西。她甚至宁愿自己没有像刚才那样做。那时她在想什么呢？

那天下午，当放学的铃声响起，乔丹觉得最好快点收拾好，以免在空荡荡的大厅里与史黛西那一小帮人狭路相逢。乔丹刚刚打开自己的储物柜，就有人从她身后将柜门重重地关上了，吓了她一跳。瞬间她便知道了这个人就是史黛西。与她如此之近的距离使乔丹呼吸困难。对于昨晚来说，这样做是个好办法，但是对于现在的情形，乔丹有些不确定。她希望自己已经坚强到可以应对史黛西做出的任何不良反应。她略带胆怯地回过头直面史黛西，默默地为她祈祷，也为自己祈求力量。

史黛西将卡片朝着乔丹的脸甩过去，责问道：“这是什么？”

“一张卡片。”对于这样一个简单的问题乔丹不假思索地回答。

史黛西像是困惑了，迟疑了一下继续说：“这真的是为我而做的？”

乔丹点点头。

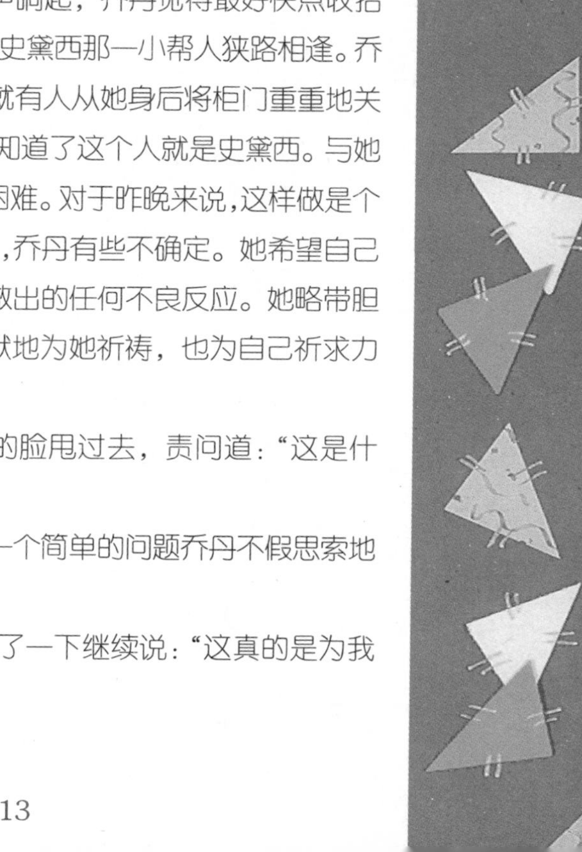

“但是为什么呢？”

乔丹微笑着指指那些用精美修饰小心翼翼写上去的文字，“你读这些字了吗？上面说我想要和你成为朋友。”

“我知道上面说了什么，”史黛西有点不耐烦，“但你是说真的吗？在我那样对待你之后……就在昨天……”

“我是说真的，史黛西。”乔丹坚定地回答她，“我不知道自己做过什么烦扰你或是冒犯你的事情，不过我很抱歉。我宁愿与你成为朋友而非敌人。我们可以做朋友吗？”

她看着史黛西近乎恭敬地用指尖轻抚着卡片。“真的很漂亮，而且花费了很多工夫。”突然间史黛西好像柔和很多，甚至有点脆弱。同情和理解在乔丹的心里滋长，她开始明白妈妈是对的，有的时候欺凌弱小者只是需要被爱。真高兴自己曾为史黛西祈祷，乔丹也为自己正确的做法感到骄傲。

“但是在发生了昨天的事情之后，” 史黛西咕咕哝哝地说，小心地回避着乔丹的双眼，“我对你如此恶劣。”

“史黛西，我原谅你。”乔丹的话让史黛西如释重负。

史黛西紧张地看着乔丹：“我想和你交朋友。”

乔丹开怀地笑起来：“太好了！也许哪天我可以让你看看我是怎么做剪贴画的。”

“我很想看。”史黛西第一次放松了紧张的神经，微笑道，“明天午餐时间我们聊聊这个好吗？也许我可以和你坐在一起。”

乔丹咧嘴一笑，点点头。“那就太好了！”突然她意识到大厅里已经没有其他学生了。她看看手表：“呀！很晚了。我妈妈还在等我。她可能会以为我在这里遇上袭击之类的了。”她再次朝史黛西笑笑，“明天见……朋友！”

史黛西微笑着。乔丹看出，那是善良美好的微笑。

乔丹挥手再见，冲向门口，代数课本被紧紧抱在胸前，可以感觉得到她心脏的剧烈跳动。她几乎要承受不住激动的心情。她不仅用创造性的才华找到了自己的定位，还用它鼓舞了他人。她已经迫不及待地要告诉妈妈了。

Chapter 5

Reviving Old Feelings

5

拯救往昔时光

Remember your history and your heritage. Reflect on the good things in your life. Think about truth and goodness. Contemplate things that are right, pure, and lovely. Have an attitude of gratitude for all I've done for you. My faithfulness is your rock through all generations.

Blessing you,
Your God of Wonder

—from Deuteronomy 32:7; Philippians 4:8; Psalm 100:5

你追想家族史和你的上辈给你的荣光。追想你的生命里美好的事。想想真理和善行。完成正义的、纯洁的、可爱的事。我为你完成的，你当称赞。我的信实，必惠顾你的万代。

祝福你，
你的奇迹之神

——《申命记》32：7；
《腓利比书》4：8；
《诗篇》100：5

It feels good to remember happy moments from the past—your first date, your child's first steps, your father's proud face when you hit the home run.

Scrapbooks are a wonderful way to keep us from losing those happy memories. One simple picture can bring back a memory long forgotten. Journaling that moment helps us remember the details and emotions.

A scrapbook revives those forgotten moments of your past. Big things, small things—it doesn't matter. They're all right there in your scrapbook. The memory is safe and secure. And so is the feeling.

You'll smile remembering the romantic getaway you took with your husband on your second anniversary. You'll laugh seeing photos of the silly costumes you made that took first place in last year's fall festival. You'll cry sweet tears looking back at the tiny infant you held so delicately—the baby who now towers over you.

Even remembering some not-so-good moments can be beneficial. Time has a tendency to soften our perspective on negative memories. Hopefully a bad experience will seem less terrible looking back. Or maybe you'll realize how much you've grown despite that problem, or even how what seemed bad at the time worked out for the best.

Either way, memories are a blessing. Renewing them has the potential to renew a marriage, strengthen a friendship, or recharge your life.

回忆过去的美好时刻是一件愉快的事情——你的初次约会，孩子的人生第一步，以及当你打出一个漂亮的全垒打时爸爸一脸自豪的神情。

剪贴簿是一种防止我们失去那些美好时光的方式。一张简单的照片就能将我们带回到一段遗忘许久的记忆。那时的札记能够帮助我们想起许多的细节和感慨。

一本剪贴簿拯救被你遗忘的往昔时光。无论大事，还是小情——这都无所谓。它们就在你的剪贴簿里。记忆在那里很安全、很保险，还有那时的感觉。

你会微笑着回忆起结婚两周年时和老公一起浪漫潜逃。看到去年秋天过节时你亲手制作的获得头奖的愚蠢礼服，你会忍俊不禁。回头看看当你小心翼翼抱着小婴儿时留下的甜蜜泪水——那时的小宝宝现在已经长得比你还高了。

即使是想想那些并不这么美好的时刻也会令人受益匪浅。时间有一种趋势，不断软化我们对负面事件的记忆。回顾起一段不堪的经历时很有可能会觉得它已经没有那么糟了。或许你会意识到，经历了那样的问题之后你成长了不少，或者当时的苦痛已经转化为后来的美好。

不管怎样，记忆是一份祝福。更新它有着让婚姻、友情历久弥新的作用，抑或是给人生充电的巨大潜能。

When work, commitment,
and pleasure all become one
and you reach that deep well
where passion lives,
nothing is impossible.

Nancy Coey

It was only 7:30 a.m.,

and she was already

running on a short fuse.

Always

"Take a bite." Vanessa held out a spoonful of oatmeal, coaxing her ten-month-old, Haydn, to eat.

Her four-year-old son, Nathan, loaded his mouth with waffles. "Mommy, look at me! "

Watching syrup drip down his chin, Vanessa tried not to be perturbed. "OK, Nathan. Now chew it up before you choke."

It was only 7:30 a.m., and she was already running on a short fuse. Vanessa and her husband, Ricky, had stayed up late arguing—again. Lately it seemed they couldn't have a normal conversation without bringing up their finances. Vanessa was making an effort not to take it out on the kids.

"Daddy! " Nathan crowed as Ricky rushed in to grab a cup of coffee.

"Hey, buddy." Ricky said, rustling Nathan's hair with his free hand. "I'm late for work. I'll see you later." He knelt down and planted a kiss on each of his sons' foreheads. Without looking Vanessa in the eyes, he brushed a kiss past her cheek, hardly making contact.

Vanessa didn't even attempt to return the gesture. Scooping another serving into Haydn's mouth, she called out, "Have a good day." But Ricky had already walked out of the back door.

She felt a little guilty still holding onto a grudge from last night. They just never had learned how to fight nicely. An argument that had begun about bills had digressed to complaints about in-laws and finally to a list of each other's personal bad habits. She had to admit it had gotten ugly. But he'd been as hurtful as she'd been, she reasoned.

Vanessa didn't have a hard time staying mad at Ricky. He had it easy. He went to work eight hours a day, five days a week. Meanwhile, Vanessa stayed at home with the kids seven days a week. She cooked, cleaned, and disciplined at all hours of the day and night. It was hard work, and she felt unappreciated.

Last night's argument had started when Ricky saw how much money she'd spent that week. Not only had Vanessa bought groceries, she'd purchased a few too many items Ricky considered "nonessentials," including more album making supplies.

His criticism always caused Vanessa to become extremely defensive. Her scrapbook time was used productively to make something the whole family would enjoy and treasure for generations to come.

"Mommy, I'm done." Nathan was standing up in his chair. At the last moment, he decided it would be much more fun to jump than to climb down. He hadn't noticed the cup of milk perched dangerously close to the table's edge.

"Nathan! " Vanessa warned, a bit too late. The cup bounced onto the floor, splattering milk everywhere.

Still in his crouched landing position, Nathan looked timidly over his shoulder. "Oops."

Vanessa pointed to the living room. "Go play," she commanded. Nathan went, dejected.

Getting down on all fours, Vanessa wiped up the mess, as she always did. Clearly she needed a vacation. She and Ricky would celebrate their tenth anniversary next week, but they just didn't have the money to take a trip this year. Actually, they hadn't taken a trip for just the two of them since before Nathan was born.

Vanessa thought back to the early years before they had children. They both worked full time, so they always had plenty of money to celebrate their anniversaries. They'd loved traveling to foreign countries, sight-seeing, and learning about other cultures. When Vanessa decided to be a stay-at-home mom, losing her income meant they'd have to forgo the exotic, romantic getaways.

"It's probably best that we don't go on a trip this year," she grumbled to herself. "We'd probably end up fighting the whole time anyway."

As she tossed a handful of soggy paper towels into the trash, Nathan bounded energetically back into the kitchen. "Mommy, can I paint?"

Vanessa sighed wearily. She hadn't even cleaned up breakfast, and he already wanted to make another mess. "No, honey, not right now."

"Will you push me in the swing outside?" he asked hopefully.

Watching Haydn spread a handful of mush through his hair, Vanessa felt defeated. "Can you please let me clean up the kitchen first?"

But Nathan was relentless. "Can we play cards?"

"Nathan, go into the other room," she said firmly. "Now." It took everything in her power to keep from shouting the words.

Having cleaned up the kitchen and little Haydn, Vanessa put him down for his morning nap. "Nathan, I'm ready to play now," she called. She knew it was hard for her older son to adjust to limited mommy time after being the center of attention for the first three years of his life.

She found him sitting on the floor, looking at family scrapbooks—something he was only allowed to do with adult supervision. He had wrinkled pages and damaged photos one too many times.

Instead of rebuking him yet again, though, Vanessa sat on the sofa. "Do you want to look at the pictures together?"

With a solemn nod, Nathan held out the scrapbook and snuggled close to Vanessa. She noticed that the scrapbook he'd chosen was one of the older ones. "Honey, this book doesn't have any pictures of you in it. These pictures were taken before you were born. Do you want to pick a different one?"

Nathan shook his head. "No, I want this one."

Having no energy to persuade him otherwise, she opened the book. Nathan pointed to the page he'd been looking at. "Mommy, whose dog is that?"

Vanessa smiled at the mutt she and Ricky had adopted from a shelter long ago. It had been their test to see if they were ready to settle down, stay close to home, and assume responsibility for another living being. After six months they'd returned the dog to the shelter and decided they were definitely not ready.

The next page featured a costume party she and Ricky had hosted. "Who's that man, Mommy?" Nathan pointed to a shot of Ricky dressed in a Zorro costume.

"That's your daddy." Vanessa chuckled at his surprised expression, then pointed to her younger self dressed as a senorita. "And that's Mommy."

"Wow; you look pretty—like a princess! "

Vanessa laughed softly and kissed the top of Nathan's head. "Thanks, sweetie."

She realized he'd never seen his parents dressed up in such flashy costumes. *We used to be so spontaneous,* she remembered ruefully. *So fun and full of love. It really is a shame we're not like that anymore.*

Even after Nathan tired of the pictures and turned his attention to watching through the window as a utility worker vented water from the hydrant on the comer, Vanessa continued flipping through the books. She hadn't looked at some of these albums in years. She had almost forgotten so many things. She was grateful she'd put the scrapbooks together so she could once again remember things they had done as a family, emotions and feelings that had long lain dormant.

She saw Ricky as he had been then. Perhaps more importantly, she saw him as she had seen him then—through eyes of true love and affection. It almost startled her when she looked at the most recent photos of their family—and noticed that Ricky really hadn't changed. Oh, he had a little less hair, and his middle wasn't quite as trim as it had once been. But now that she had seen Ricky through the old Vanessa's eyes, she could no longer see him in any other way.

Money hadn't been the source of their happiness in the past, she realized, and it shouldn't be now. Suddenly she could hardly wait to see Ricky again.

She had to see which picture of him—and their life together—was real.

Grabbing the phone, she punched in Ricky's office number. She held her breath, waiting for him to pick up.

"Hi, Ricky," Vanessa said timidly.

"Hey, babe." Ricky sounded as if he'd been waiting for her call.

"I just wanted to tell you I'm sorry for the hurtful things I said last night. I love you, and I'm happy with our life ... even if we don't have a lot of money," Vanessa admitted sincerely.

Before he answered, Vanessa heard Ricky release the breath he'd been holding. "I'm sorry too. You know that's all I really want—for our little family to be happy." He added, "And that we have food and a roof over our head."

"I am happy," Vanessa reassured him, choosing to ignore what she would usually interpret as a jibe about her spending. "Even if I don't always act like it."

For a moment an awkward, hopeful silence hung

between them. "Ricky, I thought maybe my mom could keep the kids this weekend. We could spend a quiet weekend at home, maybe watch old movies and play card games like we used to?"

"That sounds like fun! "

"And Ricky..."

"Yes?"

"I want us to go through the old scrapbooks together. I think it'd be good for us to remember some important things together—like how much we love each other and what's really significant."

"I never forgot," he reassured her.

"I guess I never did either. Ricky?"

"Yes, babe?"

"Let's always remember, OK?"

"Always."

hugs

直到永远

“吃一口，”瓦内萨举着一汤匙的燕麦，哄着10个月大的小儿子海登吃饭。

而旁边，4岁的大儿子内森，却在嘴里塞满了华夫饼干，嘟嘟囔囔地嚷嚷，“妈咪，看我！”

瓦内萨扭头看到内森的脸颊上正在往下滴着糖浆，她尽量不让自己发火。“好了，内森。现在赶紧把饼干吞下去，别噎着自己。”

这时才刚刚早上7:30，而她已经想要发火了。瓦内萨和她的丈夫里奇昨天晚上争执到很晚——而这也不是第一次了。近来，他们之间似乎根本就没有过心平气和的谈话，只要一说话，就必定会提及收入问题，之后就是争吵。瓦内萨现在尽量不把一肚子的气恼撒在孩子们身上。

里奇这时急吼吼地跑进厨房拿咖啡，“爹地！”内森大声地招

呼爸爸。

“嘿，伙计。”里奇说着，腾出一只手来挠了挠内森的头发。“我今天要迟到了。迟些见。”他跪下来，在每个儿子的额头上草草地吻了一下；接着又草草地在妻子的脸颊上吻一下，他甚至都没有看妻子的眼睛，这简直算不得是种交流。

而瓦内萨则压根儿就没打算回吻一下。她一边喂海登吃饭，一边大声说着，“祝你好运。”但这时，里奇都已经从后门出去了。

她其实还是有些内疚的，因为自己仍然揪着昨晚的事争执不放。他们从来都不懂得如何化解争吵的尴尬。昨晚开始的时候是就账单引起的争执，结果就转变成了对彼此家庭的指责，最后干脆互相罗列彼此的恶习。她现在回想起来，觉得这场争执实在是有点过分。但是她转念一想，又觉得他其实和她一样出语伤人，心里又有些不平。

瓦内萨把火都发在里奇身上，也不是没有道理的。里奇的日子确实要比她过得舒服多了：他每天工作8个小时，一周工作5天；而瓦内萨则成天都得在家带孩子。她又是煮饭，又是清扫，还要管教孩子，每时每刻都不能休息。家务活实在是太辛苦了，而且她觉得自己的工作得不到任何肯定。

昨晚的争执起始于里奇。里奇想知道她这一周的支出，结果就发现瓦内萨除了购买日常用品外，还买了一些他认为是“根本没必要的”物品，例如那些相册贴纸。

瓦内萨一听到丈夫的批评，气就不打一处来。她精心编排相册其实是为了让全家人能更好地欣赏共处的欢乐时光，而且还很有收藏价值，应该是难得的珍宝才对。

“妈咪，我吃完了。”内森说着就从椅子里站起身来。站起来后，他就觉得不如从座位里跳出来，那肯定比规规矩矩地走出来要好玩多了。然而，他没看见桌子边上正颤颤巍巍地摆着一杯牛奶。

“内森！” 瓦内萨的警告晚了一些——那个杯子应声落地，牛奶溅了一地。

内森这时仍然保持着落地的姿势，怯生生地扭头说道：“哎呀。”

瓦内萨指着卧室命令道：“去那里玩。”内森很不情愿地进去了。

瓦内萨趴在地上，仔细地把厨房的地板擦干净；她一向爱干净。是的，她确实需要放个假了。下周她和里奇就该庆祝10周年结婚纪念日了，但是今年他们实在拿不出钱去旅游。事实上，在内森还没出世前，他们就不再出去旅游了。

瓦内萨接着回想起孩子出世前的日子。那时，他俩都有工作，也能拿出足够的钱来庆祝每个纪念日。他们那时十分喜欢去外国旅行、观光、了解异地的文化。然而当瓦内萨决定放弃工作，做一名全职家庭主妇的时候，他们就不得不放弃那种充满异乡情调的、浪漫的生活方式了。

正当她把一坨湿透了的纸巾扔进垃圾桶时，内森又精力充沛地蹦回厨房，问道，“妈咪，我能画画吗？”

瓦内萨疲惫地叹了一口气。她还没来得及清理早餐桌呢，而他都已经要开始制造另一份垃圾了。“不行，亲爱的，现在还不行。”

“那你能和我一起玩荡秋千吗？”他充满希望地又问道。

这时，海登往头发里洒了一汤匙的浓粥，瓦内萨觉得自己完全没辙了。“你能先帮我清扫厨房吗？”

但是内森还是不依不饶，“那我们能玩牌吗？”

“内森，去别的房间玩，”她的语气很严厉，“现在就去。”她现在是尽量压抑着自己不要冲着孩子大吼大叫。

清扫完厨房，又把小海登弄干净之后，瓦内萨哄着海登睡着了。“内森，现在我可以陪你玩了，”她说。她知道其实大儿子才三岁而已，然而就得和弟弟一起分享妈咪的时间，并且不再是大家注意的焦点了，这确实有些难受。

她看到内森坐在地板上，正在看家庭相册——本来他是不可以单独一个人翻弄相册的。他之前曾把相册翻页弄得皱巴巴的，而且还曾毁坏过相片。

然而，这次，瓦内萨却没有责怪他，相反的，她坐到沙发上，“你想和我一起看相片吗？”

内森非常严肃地点点头。他拿着相册，朝瓦内萨爬过去。她注意到他拿在手里的是最旧的一本相册。“亲爱的，这一本还没有你的相片。拍这些相片的时候,你还没有出世呢。你想看看别的相册吗?”

内森摇摇头,“不,我就想看这本。”

她也没精力再去说服他,于是就打开相册。内森指着他之前一直在看的那页,问道,“妈咪,这是谁的狗?”

瓦内萨看着这张相片,不禁微笑起来,这是很久以前她和里奇合养的一只大狗。他俩想试试看他们是否已经准备好了过安稳的生活;是否已经能够组建一个家庭;是否可以承担起抚养新生命的责任。结果6个月后,他们把这只狗还给了领养中心,认为自己根本就没有准备好。

下一页,是她和里奇共同举办的一次化装舞会。“这个男人是谁,妈咪?”内森指着里奇打扮成佐罗的一张相片问道。

“那是你的爹地啊,”瓦内萨看到儿子惊讶的表情,忍不住笑出了声。她又指着自己那张打扮成淑女的相片,说道,“那是妈咪。”

“哇哦,你看起来好美——就像公主一样!”

瓦内萨轻轻地笑了,吻了吻内森的头顶,“谢谢你,甜心。”

她突然意识到,其实儿子从未见过自己的父母打扮成那么花里胡哨的样子。然而我们过去却时常打扮成这样啊,她有些失落地想到。那时的生活多么有趣,充满了爱意。我们现在变成这样真叫人寒心。

后来,内森都已经对相片失去了兴趣,转而开始注意看街角的清洁工人从消火栓里放水；然而，瓦内萨却还在翻看相册。她已经有好多年没看过这本相册了。她几乎忘记了这一切曾经发生过。现在她觉得很庆幸，自己能想到把所有的相册都放在一起，这样才有机会再次重温在一起的美好时光，没有让这些记忆白白流逝。

她温柔地注视着里奇的相片，就好像他在她面前一样。也许更应该说，她注视着里奇的相片，就好像她曾经那么热切地注视着他一样——用珍爱的眼光注视着他。看到最近拍的全家福时，她几乎吃了一惊——她注意到里奇几乎没有变过。哦，也许他的头发少了些，腰也粗了些，但是现在她是在用昨日的瓦内萨的眼光在看他，而且她不会再用别的方式欣赏他。

她意识到，在过去的日子里，他们从未因为金钱争执过；那么现在他们也不应该因为金钱而争吵。突然，她觉得自己特别想见到里奇。她真的很想看看如今的他——以及他俩在一起的生活——和以前的哪张相片最为相似。

于是，她抓过电话，急急忙忙地拨通了里奇的电话。她屏住呼吸，等着他拿起电话。

“嗨，里奇，”瓦内萨怯生生地说。

“嘿，宝贝，”里奇的声音听起来似乎一直在等待她的电话。

“我只是想告诉你，昨晚我说的那些话，对不起。我爱你，对我们的生活我也感到很幸福……哪怕我们没什么钱。”瓦内萨恳切地说。

他没有回答，但是瓦内萨听见他松了一口气。“我也很抱歉。你知道我最希望的是什么——就是希望我们的小家庭能够幸福快乐。”他接着又说道，“我们有食物吃，有房子住，就足够了。”

“我很幸福，”瓦内萨答道，她不再把这种话语理解成是对自己开销的微词。“即使有时我表现得好像很不满，其实我很幸福。”

有那么一小会儿，他俩都沉默着；那是有些笨拙，但却充满了希望的沉默。“里奇，我想我母亲也许愿意这个周末帮我们看孩子。我们可以在家里度过一个安静的周末，在一起看看老电影，或是玩纸牌游戏，就像以前那样。”

“听起来不错！”

“还有，里奇……”

“嗯？”

“我想和你一起看看以前的老照片。我觉得能在一起回忆以前的日子会很美好——可以回想起我们有多么相爱，可以回想起那些对我们而言特别有意义的事情。”

“那些事是我永生难忘的，”他说道。

“我猜我也永生难忘。里奇？”

“什么，宝贝？”

“我们永远记住那些美好的往事，好吗？”

“直到永远。”

Chapter 6

Protecting What's Important

6
珍藏回忆

Don't settle for survival—I've designed you for abundant life! Because I'm your refuge, your strength, and your ever-present help in times of trouble, you don't have to fear anything. Seek Me and My ways first, and I'll take care of all the rest. Keep a balanced perspective on the things that make an eternal difference.

Looking out for you,
Your Protecting Father

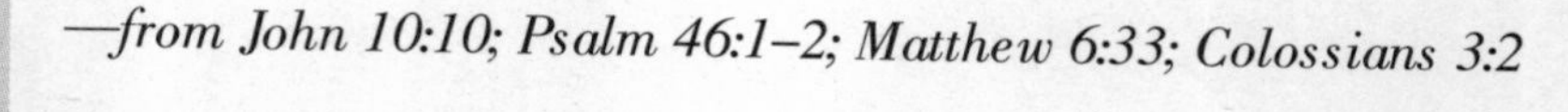

—from John 10:10; Psalm 46:1–2; Matthew 6:33; Colossians 3:2

不要懒得动弹——我已让你的生命丰盛!因我是你的避难所、是你的力量、是你在患难中随时的帮助,所以你无所畏惧。寻我和我的路,我将负责余下的事。不要忽视那些必将带来改变的事情。

为你瞭望,
你的守候之父

——《约翰福音》10:10;《诗篇》46:1-2;
《马太福音》6:33;《歌罗西书》3:2

Your scrapbooks are one of the most valuable items you own. Sure, you could get more money if you sold an antique armoire or an expensive automobile, but your scrapbooks hold so much more intrinsic value.

Besides your family and friends themselves, scrapbooks featuring your loved ones are the next closest in worth. Between those pages lie the images of your loved ones, the unique expressions and features they had at one specific moment in time. People constantly change, but photos capture and document life.

How else would the next generation believe your story about the terrible haircut your big sister gave you in high school? Or how you really did glow after delivering that ten-pound baby? Those are moments worth reliving time and time again.

The owner of a new sports car waxes and shines his investment. Special care is taken when handling fine jewelry. This is the regard we should have for our family photos, because unlike those other things, they are irreplaceable. Your family and the memories you've created together are special and worth protecting. Organizing your photos and preserving them does just that.

For you and your family, those scrapbooks—and the joy, laughter, and pain they memorialize—are priceless.

Treat them with care.

你的剪贴簿是你的所有财产中最有价值的一项。当然，如果你卖掉古董衣橱或者名贵汽车，你会赚上一大笔，但是，剪贴簿里蕴含着更丰富的内涵。

除了你的家人和朋友本身，集合了你所爱之人的特写照片的剪贴簿，就是最应珍视的了。页面上到处是你爱的人，是他们在某个特殊时刻独一无二的表情特征。

人在时刻成长变化，但是照片抓住并储存下了生活片段。

还有什么东西能让下一代相信中学时姐姐曾经给你剪过糟糕的发型？或者产下一个10磅重的宝宝时你

是多么的容光焕发?那些都是值得一次又一次重新体验的时刻。

一辆新跑车的主人总是会给车打蜡抛光。手持名贵珠宝的人们也会格外小心。同理,这就是我们对家庭相册应有的重视,因为与其他东西相比,这些照片是不可替代的。你的家人和你们一同创造的记忆是与众不同的,值得保护起来。整理照片并妥善保管就是这个目的。

对于你和家人,那些剪贴簿——还有其勾起的喜悦、欢笑和痛苦——都是无价的。

用心呵护吧。

It is the mark of great people
to treat trifles as trifles
and important matters as important.
Doris Lessing

Bob caught Debbie's eye, and his expression was grim. "It doesn't look good so far."

The Shelter

"Oh, excuse me," Debbie said, having stumbled over a man reclining on the floor. The man pulled his legs toward his chest to let her pass. She took wide strides to avoid invading anyone else's personal space. There were people everywhere—sitting, standing, and lying down. Step by awkward step, she led her family to the other side of the high-school gymnasium, trying to find adequate space to set up camp.

She nodded to her husband, Bob, signaling that she'd found a spot. He and their teenagers, Alayna and Aiden, unloaded their bags at the designated

area and together assessed their situation. They stood amid groups of people huddling, lounging, and sleeping, and felt a little uncomfortable. This would be their home for the next few days as they—along with several hundred other families—took refuge from the fast-approaching hurricane.

Just yesterday a tropical storm that was heading along the Florida coastline took an unexpected turn. Becoming fiercer than previously forecast, it was now a hurricane with winds reaching up to 110 miles per hour. Everyone along their stretch of the Florida coast had been advised to seek shelter immediately. They'd been given only two hours to board up all their windows and gather their belongings before the civil authorities had warned it would no longer be safe to remain.

The West Hills High School gymnasium was one of the makeshift shelters provided. Scanning their temporary residence, Aiden spotted a friend from school. "Hey, Mom, can I go talk to Matt?"

There wasn't much else to do. "Sure, honey."

Alayna wasn't handling their arrangement quite as well. "Mom, this is so weird! Couldn't we just find a hotel or something?"

Debbie had wished the same thing more than a few times. "I'm sorry, sweetie, but every hotel is full for three hundred miles. Everyone had to leave their homes." She stroked her daughter's long, brown hair and tried to placate her. "Let's just hope we don't have to stay too long and that the storm doesn't do as much damage as they predict."

Bob caught Debbie's eye. He had tuned his hand-held radio to a local weather station, and his expression was grim. "It doesn't look good so far," he said softly.

Hurricane weather was a new experience for the Coopers. Bob's work had brought them from California to Florida two years earlier. Since then they'd had just one other encounter with a severe hurricane. Fortunately that storm had only done minor roof damage to their house. This time it seemed they wouldn't be so lucky. They could only hope they'd

have a home to which they could return.

With nothing to do but sit and wait for the storm to pass, Debbie felt restless. She could see Alayna was reacting similarly, pacing back and forth, her brow furrowed. Debbie could tell she was in deep thought. "What's on your mind, Alayna?"

Her daughter turned to face her. "What if my music-box collection gets ruined? I'll be so upset. And what about my prom dress?"

Debbie had already lamented over the possibility of losing the new bedroom suite she'd recently purchased, but she was trying to keep a positive attitude for her family. "They're just things," Debbie tried to comfort her daughter. "We'd be sad to lose them, but we can replace them if we have to."

Suddenly Debbie remembered something that couldn't be replaced—that she could hardly bear the thought of losing. *Oh no! The scrapbooks!* If she'd only had more time, she would have brought them to ensure that they'd be protected. A queasy feeling overtook her as she thought of all the time and effort

she'd put into preserving their family photos, only to realize they might be destroyed in the hurricane. She decided not to mention it to Alayna. Mother and daughter enjoyed scrapbooking together, and she didn't want to give Alayna cause to fret even more.

Together they sat, silent in remorse over their potential losses. It took several hours before Debbie finally realized she was being self-centered. Hundreds of people in the gym were in the same situation. Everyone in the room would probably experience some loss from the hurricane, and there were hundreds of shelters just like this one with hundreds, thousands of people in the same predicament. The sheer magnitude of the potential loss changed her perspective a bit. With forced optimism she attempted to look outward instead of focusing on her own situation.

"There are lots of things I hope we still have when we get back home," Debbie said to Alayna and Bob, but mostly to herself. "Just remember, we're not the only ones being evacuated from the storm."

She nodded toward their neighbors all around them.

Alayna nodded but sounded defensive. "I know—but I'd take a California earthquake over a Florida hurricane any day! "

■

After four long, anxious nights, the Coopers were given permission to return to their home. The main highway had finally been cleared and was open for travel. As they feared, their neighborhood had been hit hard. Only residents were allowed to enter the area. Three people who had refused to evacuate had been killed in the storm.

With a mixture of anticipation and dread, the Cooper family drove home. Along the way they stared out the windows, watching the damage to homes worsen the closer they got to their neighborhood.

Two streets from their house, a fallen tree still blocked the road, making it impassable. "OK, let's walk from here," Bob instructed the family. The street was strewn with broken tree branches and rubble. Walking toward their home, Debbie noticed the

damage done to neighboring houses. A fallen tree protruded from a huge hole in one roof. Another home looked to be in fairly good condition except for the chimney. Bricks were scattered throughout the yard. She began to feel hopeful that perhaps their home had fared equally well.

"Mom, look at that one!" Aiden exclaimed, pointing to a house that looked like it was cut in half. They could see straight into the three bedrooms along the side of the house.

With more urgency Debbie moved toward their address. If not for the number on the mailbox, she wouldn't have recognized her own home. The hurricane's fierce wind had not only taken their roof, it had swept away the whole second story.

Debbie held a hand to her mouth to muffle the whimper that threatened to escape. Bob opened his arms and pulled his family close. Silently the Coopers comforted each other, their eyes fixed on what little remained of their home.

Suddenly Debbie remembered the scrapbooks.

Hurdling debris in the yard, she ran to the house to see if by some miracle they might still be there. Entering their home, she bypassed shattered glass and found more than a foot of water standing throughout what remained of the house. Across the living room, she spotted the bookcase that had held the scrapbooks lying facedown in the water. Slowly, with a sense of total dread, she dragged her feet through the water toward the bookcase. She knew there was no chance that twenty years of their family memories could possibly have endured the storm's devastation. Seeing ruined books scattered everywhere, Debbie could no longer contain her grief for all they had lost.

By then Bob and the kids had caught up with Debbie and found her in tears. Bob put his arm around her. "What is it?" he demanded, alarmed.

"Oh, Bob, they're gone ... they're all gone—our memories, our treasures—our past! "

"We've got insurance. We can replace everything," he comforted. But Debbie knew he had

no idea what she was talking about.

"Our scrapbooks, Bob," she explained tearfully. "We can't ever replace them."

"Hey, Mom," Alayna interrupted with a shout. "Look over there!" Alayna pointed to a yellow, waterproof duffel bag floating behind the sofa. She sloshed across the room and picked it up. "Mom! It's still here!" She said triumphantly, carrying the dripping bag to her mother.

Debbie recognized the bag from their recent canoe trip but had no idea what was inside. Curious, she unzipped the large bag.

Inside were their scrapbooks, perfectly preserved!

"While you and Dad were rushing around getting ready to evacuate, I remembered that we never finished scrapbooking the pictures from our canoe trip," Alayna explained to her astonished and speechless mother. "I thought it just might help to put those photos and the scrapbooks in the waterproof bag we used on the trip. I knew I wouldn't be able to save my music-box collection, but I thought I might

be able to save something important to the whole family."

Debbie stood up and hugged Alayna, feelings of pride in her daughter, gratitude, and joy overwhelming her feelings of grief and loss. Yes, they'd lost a lot. But they still had what was most important—the things that couldn't be replaced. They had each other, and they had their memories. Those things were priceless.

避难所

“哦，不好意思！”黛比不慎绊在一个斜倚在地上的人的身上。那个人把腿收回来，抱在胸前，给她让路。她把步子跨得很大，以免再次侵犯他人的私人领地。这里到处都是人——坐着，站着，还有躺着的，密密麻麻。黛比带着家人一步步艰难地前行，走向中学体育馆的另一侧，想要找到一块合适的地方来支起他们的帐篷。

她对丈夫鲍勃点了点头，示意已经找到了一个合适的地方。鲍勃和他们的两个十几岁的孩子——阿莱娜和艾登，在那里放下背包，一起审视他们所处的环境——周围是拥挤而嘈杂的人群，有的人无所事事，有的人四处闲逛，也有人正鼾声如雷——这让他们感觉有点不自在。这里将是他们未来一段时间的“家”，因为他们与另外几百个家庭一起，正在躲避一场正急速逼近的飓风。

就在昨天，正在向佛罗里达海岸靠近的一场热带风暴意外地改变了方向，变得比起初预报的更加猛烈，成了每小时风速达到

110英里的飓风。在它可能波及的范围之内的佛罗里达居民都被建议立即寻找避难所。库珀一家也只有两个小时的时间去用栅木板加固窗户，收拾家当，因为民间的权威人士警告说，超过这个时间就不安全了。

西山中学体育馆就是临时避难所之一。审视了一遍他们的临时居所之后，艾登发现了一个校友，他对妈妈说："妈妈，我可以过去和马特聊聊吗？"

因为没有很多活要干了，黛比说："当然可以，宝贝。"

阿莱娜对这次的安排表示不解："妈妈，这好奇怪啊，我们就不能住进宾馆之类的地方吗？"

黛比也无数次地有过这样的愿望。"真是抱歉，小可怜。因为所有的居民几乎都离开了家，住到了外面，所以方圆300公里以内的宾馆房间都已经住满了。"她爱抚着女儿棕色的长发，安慰她说，"就让我们祈祷不需要在这里待很久，而且风暴造成的危害并没有想象中的那么大吧。"

这时候鲍勃的举动引起了黛比的注意——他把收音机调到了一家当地电台，表情凝重地轻声说："到目前为止，情况不容乐观。"

飓风天气对库珀一家来说是比较新鲜的经历。两年前，由于鲍勃工作变动，他带着全家从加利福尼亚来到佛罗里达。从那以后，他们只经历过一次比较强的风暴，幸运的是，那次风暴只破坏了房顶的很小一部分。而这次可能不会那么幸运了，所以他们只是希望能有一个可回之家。

除了坐等暴风雨过境，黛比现在没有别的事情可做，她感到了不安。她看到阿莱娜也有同样的反应，踱来踱去，眉头紧锁。黛比看出了女儿的焦虑，“阿莱娜，你在担心什么呢？”

她女儿转过头来说：“如果我的八音盒收藏被毁掉怎么办？我会很心疼的，还有我的舞会礼服呢？”

黛比也正暗自伤心，因为她前几天新买的卧室组合家具估计是保不住了，但是为了稳定家人的情绪，她还是强撑着表现出乐观。“那些只是些小东西罢了，”黛比开导女儿说，“失去它们我们会感到难受，但是如果需要的话，我们可以再买啊。”

突然，黛比想起了一件无可替代的东西，她将无法承受失去它所带来的痛苦。哦，不！那几本剪贴簿！要是她再有多一点点的时间，她肯定会更妥善地保护好它们的。那是一种源自心底的痛苦。黛比喜欢和女儿一起做剪贴，她们花了大把的时间收集、整理家庭相册，而她们多年的心血却很可能在这场飓风中毁于一旦。她掩饰住自己的不安，也不打算和阿莱娜提起这事，以免增加她的焦虑。

他们坐在一起，静静地为他们可能的损失暗暗担心。几个小时后黛比才猛然意识到自己是多么狭隘，总是以自我为中心。体育馆里的几百人都面临着同样的困境。同一屋檐下的每个人都要忍受飓风带来的损失，而像这里一样容纳成百上千“无家可归者”的避难所还有几百个。不可估量的巨大损失些许改变了她的视点。强作乐观的她努力将眼界放开，而非紧盯

自家的窘境。

“有好多东西都是我希望我们回家的时候还在的。”黛比对阿莱娜和鲍勃说，但更像是在说服自己。“记住，我们并不是被暴风雨赶出家门的唯一家庭。”此时，她向身边处于同样困境的人们会心一笑。

阿莱娜勉强地点点头，但是话音里带着不满：“我知道，但是真有那么一天的话，我宁愿要加利福尼亚地震而不是佛罗里达飓风。”

……

漫长而又焦虑的四天过去了，库珀一家终于接到通知，可以回家了。城市主干道已经清理干净，交通恢复正常。正如他们害怕的那样，临近区域的建筑都严重损毁。只有本地的居民才允许进入该区域。这片区域中拒绝疏散的三个人已经在暴风雨中丧生。

库珀一家人驶向家园，心中夹杂着期待与恐惧。沿途他们凝视窗外，离他们的社区越近，住宅的损毁情况就越严重。

在距离他们家两条街的地方，一棵树横倒在路中央，汽车无法通过。“好吧，让我们从这里步行回去。”鲍勃领着家人朝着家的方向走去。沿路遍布着断树枝和碎石。一路上，黛比将邻居们房子的损坏情况都看在眼里：一棵树把某家房顶戳了个大洞；有一幢房子看上去相当完好，只是烟囱已不成形，砖块散落到了整个院子里。也许自己家的房子的情况和这家的差不多，她依稀看到了希望。

“妈妈，看那个！”艾登大叫道，指向一座好像是被切成了两半的房子。他们甚至可以从房子的一侧看尽里面的三间卧室。

黛比加快了回家的脚步。要不是看到信箱上的号码，她根本认不出自己家的房子了。飓风残暴地卷走了他们的房顶，还有整个二层。

黛比用手捂住嘴，心中的绝望让她想要逃走。鲍勃张开双臂，将家人抱拢在一起。一家人在无声中相互支持，目光不约而同地锁定在那片家的残骸上。

突然，黛比想起了剪贴簿。跨过院子里的残垣断壁，她跑进房子去找那些剪贴簿，并暗自祈祷它们会奇迹般地留存下来。进入房子，她绕过散落的碎玻璃，发现屋里剩下的东西都浸泡在一英尺深的水里。穿过卧室，她一眼看见了装着剪贴簿的书柜底朝天漂在水面上。她恐惧极了，慢慢地涉水向书柜走去。她意识到这保存了20年家庭记忆的一份记录已经不太可能在这场暴风雨中平安留存了。眼见着到处散落的书，黛比再也抑制不住痛失这一切的悲痛。

这时候，鲍勃和孩子们也赶了过来，发现她已泪流满面。鲍勃抱住她问：“怎么回事？”

“噢，鲍勃，都没有了……一切都没有了——我们的记忆，我们的宝贝，我们的过去！”

“我们还有保险。我们可以重新置备一切。”他安慰道。黛比知道，他并不明白她到底指的是什么。

“我们的剪贴簿，鲍勃。”她含泪说道，“我们不可能重新置备它们啊。”

“哦，妈妈，”阿莱娜喊着打断她，“看那里！”阿莱娜指向一个沙发后面浮着的黄色防水粗呢袋子。她涉水过去把它捡了起来。“妈妈，它还在这！”她狂喜地把滴着水的袋子递给妈妈。

黛比认出这个袋子曾用于不久前的一次独木舟旅行，但是想不起来里面是什么东西了。她好奇地打开这个大袋子。

里面正是他们的剪贴簿，保存得完好无损！

“你和爸爸急着准备疏散的时候，我想起我一直没有把我们滑独木舟旅行的照片整理进剪贴簿。”阿莱娜向吃惊到说不出话的妈妈解释说，“我想，把照片和剪贴簿都放进我们旅行时用的袋子应该会比较保险。我知道我无法保住我收藏的八音盒，但是我想我也许能够保住一点对全家人都很重要的东西。”

黛比站了起来，抱住了女儿，为女儿而感到骄傲。心中的感激和欣慰，冲淡了她的痛苦和失落。的确，他们失去了很多，但是他们还保有最为重要的东西——一些无可替代的东西。他们拥有彼此，他们拥有那份记忆，而这些才是最珍贵的。

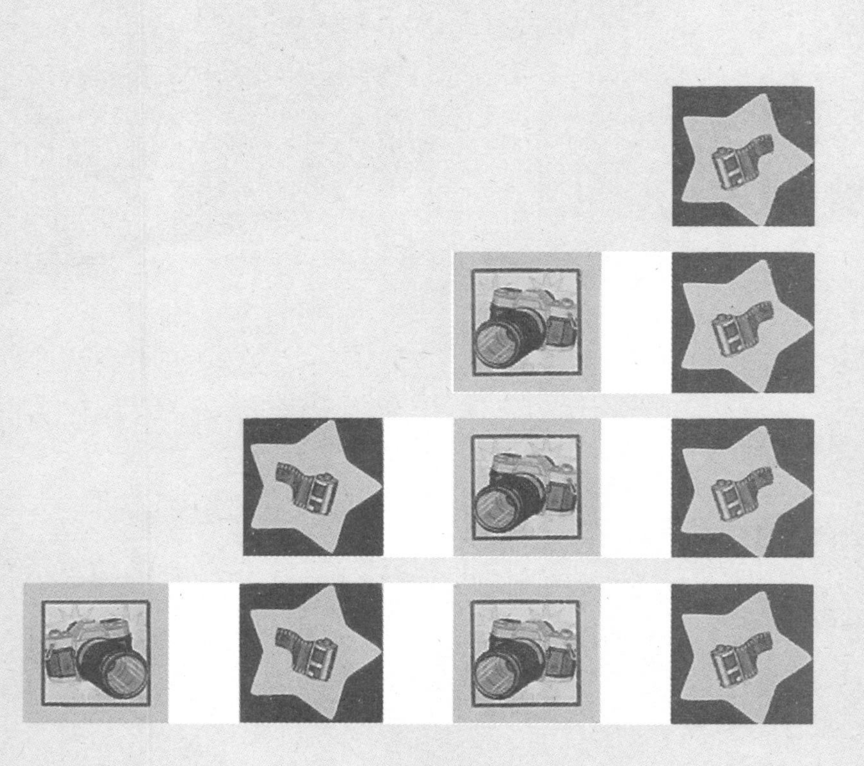

Chapter 7

Giving Love

7 爱的付出

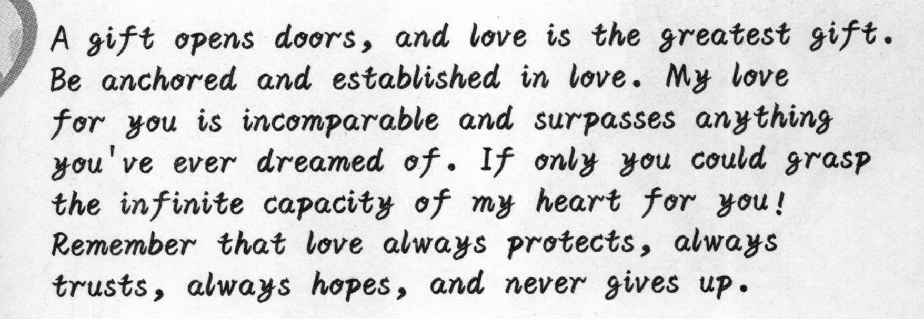

A gift opens doors, and love is the greatest gift. Be anchored and established in love. My love for you is incomparable and surpasses anything you've ever dreamed of. If only you could grasp the infinite capacity of my heart for you! Remember that love always protects, always trusts, always hopes, and never gives up.

With unfailing affection,
Your God of Love

—from Proverbs 18:16; Corinthians 13:13; Ephesians 3:17–19; Corinthians 13:7

人的礼物为他开路，爱是最好的礼物。我对你的爱无可比拟，超越你能想到的一切。但愿你能明白我的爱！记住——凡事包容、凡事相信、凡事盼望、凡事忍耐。

永远深情的，

爱之神

——《箴言》18：16；《歌林多前书》13：13；《以弗所书》3：17—19；《歌林多前书》13：7

Scrapbooking is a labor of love. The people gracing the pages of your scrapbook are your family and friends. They're the ones who impact your life enough to make you want to photograph them in the first place. The fact that you put them in your book signifies that they are the people for whom you truly care. The countless hours you spend cropping photos and decorating pages shows how much you value those people. Children especially love to look at pictures of themselves. How often does a mother hear her child's request, "Mom, take my picture! " Their reward (and yours) is holding the photo in

inspirational message

hand and marveling at their image. Children may understand even more than adults the clear message of love when someone wants to take their picture. And even more love and value is perceived when someone takes the time and care to showcase those photos in a handcrafted scrapbook.

You communicate love by scrapbooking. Your work demonstrates unquestionably that the people whose activities and accomplishments you chronicle are worth your valuable time and effort. And demonstrating your love for someone is the most important gift of all.

剪贴簿是爱的付出，那些为你的剪贴簿增光添彩的人都是你的亲人和朋友，这些人在你的生命中深深影响着你，你要首先留下他们的影像。你能够将其加入你的剪贴簿，说明他们是你真心在乎的人。你花在裁剪照片和装饰页面上的无数个小时表明了你对他们的珍视。

孩子们尤其喜欢看自己的照片。妈妈常常可以听到孩子要求道：“妈妈，给我照相！”他们的奖励（还有你的）就是手

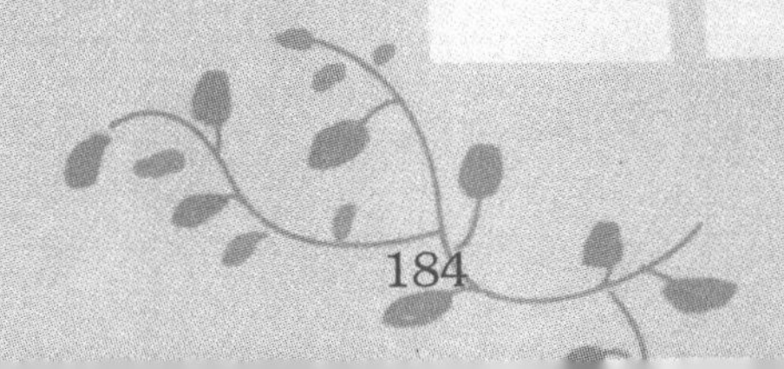

持照片，新奇地欣赏自己照片中的形象。当有人想要给他们照相时，孩子们可能对这条爱的简讯比大人们理解得更深。当有人舍得花时间和心思，在手工制作的剪贴簿中展示这些照片，那就会有更多的爱和珍视被记录下来。

剪贴簿可以交流彼此的爱。你的成果无疑证明，编入剪贴簿的人们的活动和成就是值得你花上宝贵的时间和努力的。同时也证明，你对某人的爱是最重要的礼物。

Those gifts are ever the most acceptable
which the giver has made precious.
Ovid

Jessica had held herself

together until that

moment. But suddenly

words gave way to tears of

stress and exhaustion.

The Blessing

Jessica closed her eyes and rested her head on the kitchen counter, waiting for relief from her throbbing headache. She pressed her temples and debated whether to push through her exhaustion and handle the chores she had planned for the day or give up and take a nap.

A rap at the back door ruled out that option. Slowly she raised her head to see her best friend, Lori, wave through the window and let herself in. Lori was always bubbly and energetic, but she toned her mood down immediately when she got a good look at Jessica. She sat on the kitchen stool beside her friend. "Hey, Jessica. How'd it go last night?"

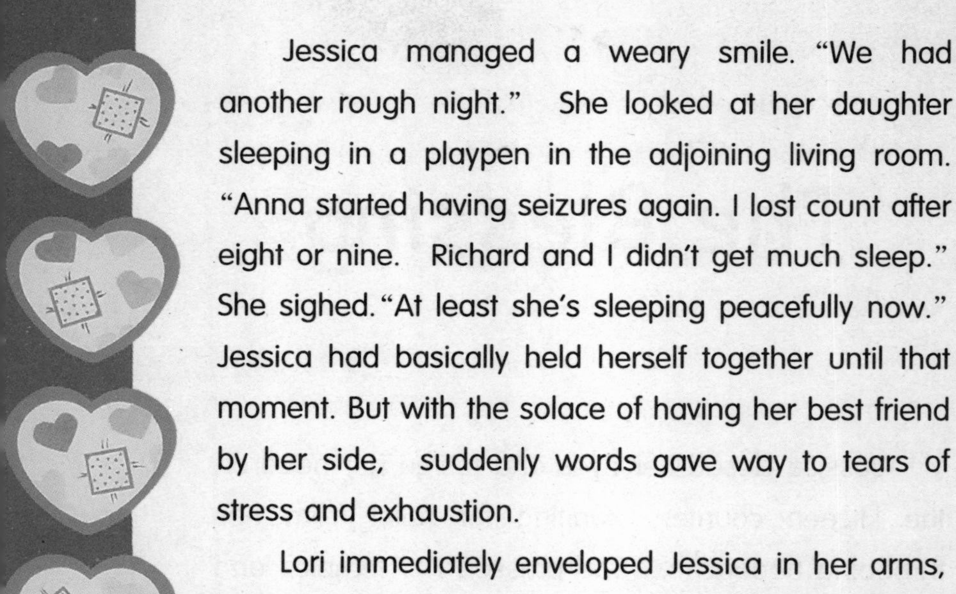

Jessica managed a weary smile. "We had another rough night." She looked at her daughter sleeping in a playpen in the adjoining living room. "Anna started having seizures again. I lost count after eight or nine. Richard and I didn't get much sleep." She sighed. "At least she's sleeping peacefully now." Jessica had basically held herself together until that moment. But with the solace of having her best friend by her side, suddenly words gave way to tears of stress and exhaustion.

Lori immediately enveloped Jessica in her arms, holding on tight. "I'm so sorry, Jessica. You should have called me. I would have been right over to help."

Jessica shook her head. "I'm just so tired of asking for help. It's been ten months of others helping us. I feel indebted to the whole world."

Lori pulled away and looked Jessica straight in the eye, reprimanding the girl she'd known since elementary school. "You should have called me."

Jessica nodded repentantly and smiled slightly

but more genuinely this time.

Lori tucked loose strands of hair behind Jessica's ear. "Why don't you get some rest while I do a few things around the house? I'll wake you up if anything happens with Anna. OK?"

Jessica let out a sigh of relief and gratitude. "Thanks, Lori. I don't know what I'd do without you."

Jessica had conceived after many years of infertility. But the initial joy at this news had been quickly overshadowed by fear when tests verified that the baby would be severely retarded and would likely have a host of other disorders.

Although early tests indicated that Anna was not as mentally challenged as they'd expected, she was born with heart defects that required several surgeries to remedy. She was subject to chronic infections and had recently started having seizures. Her little life had started roughly, and it didn't seem to be getting any better. Jessica's initial hopefulness was fading into despair that her baby wouldn't survive to her first birthday—another of the dire

predictions.

"Lori, sometimes I just don't think I can handle this. She's so sick! Every day I wonder if it may be the day her little heart decides to quit. Then I wonder why God would let this happen in the first place! " She couldn't hide the tinge of anger she felt.

Lori was quiet for a minute, then she took Jessica's hand and led her to Anna's playpen. Together they looked over the frail child. Lori knelt and tenderly caressed Anna's forehead. "Jessica, I know it may not feel true right now, but God promises He won't give you more than you can handle." She brushed Anna's cheek with her fingertips and continued softly but confidently. "Look at her, Jessica. She's beautiful! " She looked up at her friend, and Jessica saw the tears that were filling her eyes too.

"God created Anna, and I have no doubt He has a plan for her little life." Lori stood and took Jessica's hands, looking her in the eyes with conviction. "We don't know how long we'll have Anna with us—no one ever knows how long we'll have those we love.

So we've got to treat every day as a gift. Last night was tough. Let's pray that today will be better."

■

Later that day Lori stopped by again to check on Jessica and Anna. "How are you doing?"

Jessica smiled and kissed Anna's head as she sat cooing on her lap. "We're both doing much better."

"I'm so glad to hear it." Lori grinned and handed Jessica a completed checklist. "I finished the errands you had ... and I brought you something." She presented a small scrapbook with a ribbon holding the pages closed.

Jessica couldn't conceal her delight at the surprise. "What's this?"

Anna was already fascinated and batting at the book, and Lori laughed. "Well, it looks like Anna wants to find out, so open it."

Jessica untied the ribbon and opened the scrap-book. The first page featured a picture from Anna's first day of life. Above the photo of the tiny infant was

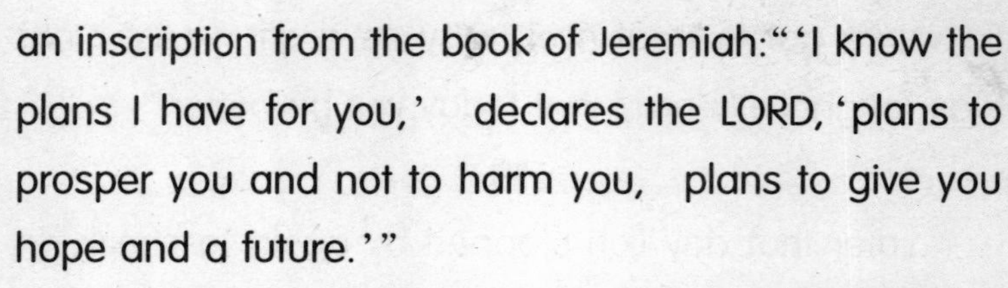

an inscription from the book of Jeremiah: " 'I know the plans I have for you,' declares the LORD, 'plans to prosper you and not to harm you, plans to give you hope and a future.' "

Each page showed the milestones of Anna's little life. Her first meeting with her parents. Her first day home after five weeks in the hospital. Her first outing to church services.

"I wanted to wait for Anna's first birthday to give it to you, but I felt you needed it now. I've been collecting photos ever since Anna was born so I could put together this scrapbook. I knew you wouldn't have time."

Jessica felt hot tears coming again, this time joyful ones. She was overwhelmed by the labor of love her dear friend had displayed. "Thank you, Lori. This is such a special gift! I'll treasure it forever."

Lori reached over and let Anna take a finger in her baby-firm grip. "*This is a special gift.* The scrapbook is so we'll never forget it, no matter what the future holds."

hugs

祝福

杰西卡闭上眼睛，把头靠在厨房的台子上，希望能借此缓和一下阵阵的头疼。她按住自己的太阳穴，考虑究竟是应该忍住疲劳，把今天的家务活都做完，还是干脆撒手去睡一小会儿。

这时有人敲后门。她慢慢地抬起头，发现是她最好的朋友来了。劳丽从窗户外向她挥手，然后自己打开门走了进来。劳丽总是话很多，而且精力旺盛，但是当她看到杰西卡这副模样时，不禁也有些压抑。她在朋友的身边坐下来，说道："嘿，杰西卡。昨晚事情还顺利吗？"

杰西卡挤出了一个疲惫的笑容。"昨晚过得很不好。"说着，她看了看隔壁卧室里正在婴儿床上酣睡的女儿。"安娜昨晚又不舒服了。到了八九点钟的时候，我都数不清她究竟发作了几次。理查德和我几乎没怎么睡。"她叹口气，"但还好，至少她现在睡得很

好。”杰西卡一直咬牙坚持到现在，但是最好的朋友此刻就在她身边，突然她就忍不住哭了，仿佛所有的压力和疲惫都一下子喷涌而出。

劳丽紧紧地把杰西卡抱在自己的怀里，“我真是为你难过，杰西卡。你昨晚应该打电话给我的。我会立即过来帮忙。”

杰西卡摇了摇头，“我都已经累得不想再喊你过来帮忙了。这10个月以来大家一直都在帮我的忙。我觉得自己欠了这整个世界很多很多。”

劳丽松开手，看着杰西卡的眼睛，责备这个她从小学时就熟悉的好朋友，“你确实应该给我打电话的。”

杰西卡有些悔意地点点头，然后又轻轻地微笑了一下，十分真诚。

劳丽帮杰西卡把头发往耳后捋了捋，“为什么你不去休息一下呢？我来帮你做家务。如果安娜有什么状况，我就把你喊醒。好吗？”

杰西卡松了口气，心怀感激。“谢谢你，劳丽。如果没有你，我该怎么办呢？”

杰西卡一直都没能怀孕。但是怀孕之后的喜悦却被一些可怕的消息冲淡了，孕期测试表明婴儿可能是严重的智障，而且还有可能患有其他一些病症。

尽管安娜出世后，智力方面并没有什么问题，但是她的心脏却有先天性缺陷，需要几次手术才能治愈。她一直受慢性感染之苦，而且最近开始发作得厉害了。她幼小的生命饱受痛苦,也没有什么康复的前景。杰西卡最初的希望现在都变成了绝望，她的宝贝可能都活不过自己一岁的生日——这是一个多么可怕的预言。

“劳丽,有时我甚至想,我根本就应付不了这一切。她病得这么厉害!每天我都在想今天会不会就得看着她离去。接着我就会想为什么上帝要让这一切发生在我的身上！”此时,她根本就无法掩饰自己的愤怒。

劳丽沉默了足足有一分钟的时间，然后她拉起杰西卡的手,牵着她走到安娜的摇篮边。她们一起俯身看着这个脆弱的生命。劳丽跪下来,轻柔地抚摸着安娜的额头。“杰西卡,我知道眼下你也许觉得很不公平，但是上帝只会给你能够负担的东西。”她用手指轻柔地抚摸着安娜的脸颊,接着说道,“看看她,杰西卡。她真美!”然后她抬起头看着自己的好朋友,杰西卡看见劳丽的眼里也满是泪水。

“上帝创造了安娜,当然也就为她安排了以后的人生。”劳丽站起身,牵起杰西卡的双手,自信地看着她的双眼,“我们都不知道安娜能和我们相处多久——没有任何人能知道究竟自己可以和爱的人相处多久。因此,我们把每一天都当成是一份崭新的礼物。昨晚的经历很糟糕,但是我们可以祈祷,愿今天比昨天好。”

◆

那天晚些时候，劳丽来看看杰西卡和安娜过得怎么样。“你们怎么样？”

杰西卡微笑着，亲吻着安娜的额头。小安娜正坐在妈妈的膝头上。“我们比昨天好多了。”

“真为你们高兴。”劳丽也笑了，递给杰西卡一个完整的清单，“我把你要完成的家务活列出来了……还给你带了一样东西。”她递过来一个小小的相册，相册的封皮上系着根彩带。

杰西卡惊喜极了，“这是什么？”

安娜也很兴奋，她用小手拍打着相册，劳丽不禁笑了起来。“嗯，好像安娜急了，快打开看看吧。”

杰西卡解开彩带，打开相册。第一页是安娜出世时的相片。安娜的相片上面是圣经里耶利米书上的一段话：“‘我知道我向你们所怀的意念，’耶和华说，‘是赐平安的意念，不是降灾祸的意念，要叫你们对未来有指望。’”

每一页都记录着幼小的安娜成长的每一步。她第一次与父母的见面。她在医院住满五周后第一次回到家里。她第一次出去参加教堂仪式。

“我本想等到安娜一岁生日那天再送给你，但是我想也许你现在就想看看。从安娜出生那天起，我就一直在收集她的相片，保存在这本相册里。我知道你没时间做这些。”

杰西卡能感觉到自己滚烫的眼泪充盈着眼眶，这是喜悦的泪水。她完全被自己好友的善意感动了。“谢谢你，劳丽。这礼物真的太珍贵了！我会永远保存的。”

劳丽伸出手，让安娜紧紧地握住。“这确实是非常独特的礼物。我们永远都不会忘记这本相册里记录的一切，不论未来带给我们的是什么。”

（鲍曼系安徽大学教师，贺爱军系宁波大学教师）

一轮落日 一泓湖水 一滴眼泪 一捧笑容
Love